EUROPEAN STONE VACATION

MÓRDHA STONE CHRONICLES, BOOK 6.5

KIM ALLRED

STORM COAST PUBLISHING, LLC

EUROPEAN STONE VACATION
Mórdha Stone Chronicles, Book 6.5
KIM ALLRED

Published by Storm Coast Publishing, LLC

Print edition January 2021
ISBN 978-1-953832-04-7
Large Print Edition April 2022
ISBN 978-1-953832-14-6

AUTHOR'S NOTE

After writing *The Heart Stone*, I knew AJ and Finn's adventure had come to an end, but the story of the stones wasn't complete. I had thought to wait a few years and perhaps pick up the threads to finish the tale with other characters. While I might have thought the series to be done, the readers had other thoughts. With that idea in my head, and perhaps with the voices of two characters that refused to be silenced, my subconscious went into overdrive and the next journey seemed so obvious. This next journey, while full of danger, will be a thrilling roller-coaster adventure driven by two people who simply seemed made for each other—although two hundred years separated them.

This novella, while initially meant to share holiday cheer with good friends, created an avenue to bridge the first six books in the series with the next ones to come. And all I can say for the next books in the series...sparks and musket balls will fly!

Enjoy!

Kim

1

Northern France - Present Day

T he wheels of the oversized suitcase bumped up the step and was dragged another foot before it was heaved up the next one. Stella Caldway repositioned her satchel, which could be mistaken for an overnight bag, and sipped coffee from the giant mug she brought from Baywood, Oregon. She tugged the suitcase closer to tackle the next step.

"Here, let me help." Finn Murphy reached for the handle and got his hand slapped for the attempt.

"I can do it." Stella pushed the strap of the satchel back onto her shoulder then pushed back her auburn hair.

"Of course, you can. But it's the holidays. Let me do something simple."

Stella laughed. "AJ has been a bit of a task master."

"Between her and Ethan, I'll need another holiday after this." Finn took the suitcase and led Stella into the villa.

"To be honest, I think your sister is almost as bad." Before Stella could reach the front door, two boys tore by her, elbowing their way through the door. A small girl tagged behind, holding onto the arm of a large stuffed tiger.

A second later, Adam Moore rushed by. "Sorry, they got away from me." He grabbed his daughter, Charlotte, and swung her up into his arms as she giggled, hitting him in the head with the tiger. "Patrick, Robbie, I told you to wait." His raised voice was quickly muffled as his footsteps receded into the estate.

Madelyn ran up the stairs, then stopped on the expansive porch and glanced around. She leaned an arm against one of the wooden columns. "I'm getting too old to run after them." She blew out a breath. "Maybe it was a mistake bringing them."

Stella, who once couldn't stand being in the same room as AJ's sister-in-law, placed a hand on the woman's arm. "Adam seems to have them well in hand." When Madelyn only winced, Stella held back a chuckle. "Or will soon. I think AJ said there was a wine cellar."

Madelyn gave Stella an appreciative look. "Thirty minutes, then meet in the kitchen?"

"Absolutely." Stella turned to Finn. "Take me to my room? I need out of these shoes."

An hour later, Stella sighed with pleasure as she sipped her wine and stared at the foreboding sea. Madelyn slumped at the other end of the table, her legs resting on a nearby chair. The dining room table was separated from the kitchen by a long counter and was positioned in front of a glass wall that provided an unimpeded view of the northern French coastline. The sky was as gray as an Oregon winter day, but the sun pushed through occasional breaks in the clouds.

"Tell me again why we selected a dreary location for the holidays? Wouldn't the south coast of France have been a better option? You know, with sun." Stella was simply making conversation. It was nice to be away, and she'd always been curious about the monastery that had become so important to AJ and her time jumps to the past. Since there wasn't a chance in hell Stella would be willing to travel to the past, everyone agreed visiting the monastery would be the closest to reliving part of AJ's travels, even if two hundred years had passed since she'd been there.

"I can come up with a couple of reasons, but we all know it's because of Maire." Finn pushed his empty beer bottle aside and returned to his tablet.

"And when are your sister, Ethan, and AJ arriving?" Stella asked. The three of them, along with Professor Emory driving the third rental car, had been given the mission of stopping to buy groceries for the ten days they'd be staying.

"I think we can expect a side trip." Helen, AJ's mother, placed a platter on the table, filled with cheese, crackers, and grapes the group had picked up at a small grocery on their way to the villa. She took a seat between Stella and Madelyn. "Emory knew the women wouldn't be satisfied unless they saw the monastery before anything else."

Stella rolled her eyes. "I thought so. Thank heavens it's only twenty minutes away."

Finn gave her an indulgent smile. "AJ promised she wouldn't spend all of her time there. I'd like to see how the town faired after all these years. I wonder if Guerin's Inn is still there."

"We could have taken the time to stop on the way in," Helen said, then shook her head with a smile as the three children raced by. "Or maybe not."

Stella had prepared for traveling with eleven other people, three of them children, but it had been more taxing than she realized. She'd considered not going along with the crazy notion of spending the holidays in France, but AJ insisted there would be plenty of girl time. The long drive from Paris was eased by having three rental cars. Adam and Madelyn had one with the kids, and the rest of the group split up in the other two cars. Finn agreed to take a carload to open up the villa they'd rented while Emory would drive the third and stop to do the week's shopping.

Finn slid the tablet aside. "I think we all knew the monastery would be of interest to Maire, AJ, and the professor. And we all agreed on group breakfasts and dinners with an exception here and there. I noticed the area has become quite well known for their cider. And we're close enough for day trips to some remarkable locations."

Adam walked in and snagged a beer from the fridge. He glanced at Finn, who nodded when Adam raised the bottle. After grabbing a second one, he dropped into a chair and slid the fresh bottle to Finn. "I'm looking forward to our overnight trip to Normandy. Are you sure you and AJ don't want to come along?"

Finn shook his head. "I wouldn't mind, but I doubt I'll be able to pry her or Maire away from the monastery for any longer than half a day." He glanced at Helen. "Besides, I think it will be a nice outing for your family and Helen. I think Emory is looking forward to it as well."

Stella smiled when Helen blushed. She'd told AJ months ago that something was up with her mother and the professor. AJ didn't agree until after the third family gathering that he attended. AJ might think it was just a casual friendship, but Stella saw something deeper. Children were always the last to know.

She turned her focus to AJ's brother, amazed to admit she'd genuinely grown to like him and Madelyn. "Well, at least everyone got past customs with their passports. You have some interesting friends, Adam."

He shook his head. "Not friends. Clients. Well-paying clients."

Everyone laughed, ignoring the illegal creation of identities, birth records, driver's licenses, and passports that Adam had produced for Finn, Ethan, and Maire.

"To Baywood's criminal underground." Adam lifted his beer.

Finn raised his bottle as he called out, "Sláinte."

And they toasted to what Stella already knew in her gut would be a holiday to remember.

———

The rental car bounced through a pothole as it turned into the mostly empty, gravel parking lot across from the main entrance to the monastery. AJ Moore stared out the window toward the old stone building. It was late afternoon and several people walked to their cars. They appeared to be the archeology staff based on their youthful college-age appearance, wearing jeans or khakis, all in hiking boots.

She glanced to Emory then to Maire, who sat in the back seat with Ethan. The plan was to wait until their meeting with Gallagher, Professor Emory's contact, which was scheduled for tomorrow, before driving to the monastery. But Maire couldn't wait. She had to see it. AJ couldn't blame her. She was curious herself how the monastery had changed in the last two hundred years. From their perspective, it had only been six months since they'd been here.

From outside, AJ was surprised how little had changed. The grounds around the building now included landscaping, a parking lot, and a new building where the stables used to be. The monastery itself seemed to be in the same condition, but when she squinted, she could see where repairs had been made over the centuries. Even now, a scaffolding had been set up on the far-left corner of the building.

Ethan and Professor Emory got out of the rental car, stopping a few short feet away to take in the sight. From inside the vehicle and through the half-opened window, the women could hear the professor as he pointed to the outer buildings, the new stables, and the outer courtyard. The courtyard where Finn had killed the Duke of Dunsmore. The professor continued on as he explained the inner courtyard they would see tomorrow. The place where Finn had been captured by the duke, and a day later Peele had been killed. An event that triggered a betrayal by his brother, Dodger, resulting in Thorn's death at Waverly.

Maire stretched her arm from the back seat to touch AJ's shoulder. She grabbed Maire's hand, and they sat in measured silence. Only those that had been here and had lived through it could understand. Maire hadn't thought it would be this hard, and she swallowed the lump in her throat.

"Did you want to get out?" AJ's voice was thick, and she released Maire's hand to reach for her water bottle.

A few minutes ticked by before Maire spoke. "I pictured myself running through the halls, eager to find all of Sebastian's favorite places." A moment later, after the sound of rustling from the back seat, she blew her nose.

AJ opened her door and turned to Maire. "Come on. Some fresh air will do us both good. Just for a few minutes, then we'll see what our villa looks like." She knew this would be harder on Maire.

They all had memories of time spent here. AJ had no desire to see the garden behind the kitchen where she'd killed Dugan with a well-placed arrow. She didn't want to remember the dank, rat-infested cell where Finn had been tortured at the hands of the duke. But it hadn't been all bad. She yearned, as she knew Maire did, to sit in Sebastian's library by the light of a lantern and listen to his stories. Or visit the room where she'd stayed, waiting for Jamie and the *Daphne* to sail into the bay. She'd felt safe among friends.

There would be time to evaluate the past. To accept and

move on. Though one or two memories would be shoved back into the dark corner they belonged. She rubbed her face and got out, slamming her door shut before opening the back passenger door and holding out a hand for Maire.

"Come on. Let's walk down and see what they did with the stables. Baby steps."

Maire gave her a withering look, and AJ smiled. "That's the spirit." AJ refused to let go of Maire's hand, and after a few steps, she pulled Maire to her so they could walk arm in arm over the gravel lot toward the outer courtyard.

Ethan and the professor followed behind, Emory's voice booming as if he were instructing his first-year students. "As I mentioned on our trip over, this is a working monastery. There aren't as many monks as there used to be, but they have volunteers and several paid staff. Their main source of income is the cider.

"When an adventurous monk found a secret passage, several old rooms were discovered, including the one with the journal, and the historical society was contacted. Soon after, the archaeologists arrived. The church is open to visitors except for evening and holiday vigils. And, of course, there's the Cider House where the stables used to be. The monks run tours two days a week during the winter, except for the holidays when they're open every day until the new year. Though many visitors aren't interested in the tour."

AJ snorted. It wasn't surprising that most came for the cider, not a lesson in history. Her father would have loved this. And he'd be vying for the chance to see the underground tunnels. How much had Gallagher discovered? How many of the tunnels were still intact?

The outer courtyard was still covered in cobblestone. To the left was the door that entered the monastery. It was now a double door with a small shed to the right. The neat, handwritten sign gave away its function as a ticket booth for monastery tours. AJ felt the ghostly touch of Beckworth's hand as he guided her past the lecherous mercenaries that fatal night. She touched her cheek that had been scratched after Beckworth had pushed her against the wall—a ploy to distract the guards. Her chest tightened as she remembered her friends.

Maire squeezed her arm, and AJ shook herself, turning to the right. The path to the stables had been restored and gardens had been added, though only a few plants were still green, the rest already dormant for the winter. A stone patio had been added where empty chairs and tables were scattered with several stored against the building.

The professor moved ahead of the group, continuing to play tour guide. "The Cider House is only open until three during the week, even this time of year. It's open until seven on weekends."

The building, twice the size from what AJ remembered, kept the original look and feel of French barns from two hundred years ago, but without the horses and carts. The women peered through the windows.

"Is this where they make the cider?" Maire rubbed the glass, trying to get a better look. "It looks like a restaurant. Is that a kitchen?"

AJ studied the open area inside the building. The interior had been decorated in keeping with the feel of a barn with antique farm equipment displayed on the walls or in corners. A separate glass-walled section was easily identifiable as a gift shop.

The professor stood next to them and curved his hands around his eyes as he peered through the window. "From what Gallagher said, the back portion of the building has been left to show what the stables would have looked like decades ago. A couple old carts have been restored and are being kept for display. I think there's one outside for the kids to play on." He pointed toward the areas Maire and AJ had already seen. "Oh yes, a nice little restaurant and gift shop. I think they plan on adding a small theater to show how the cider is made. I understand during the summer months additional gift and food carts are added outside for some of the local businesses to sell their wares. Just marvelous."

The professor's words faded as AJ strolled with Maire to the rock wall that protected the courtyard from the cliff. The bracing wind blew across the bay and the women huddled closer, their hair flying behind them. For an instant, AJ stood on the bow of the *Daphne* as they crossed the Channel, the salt air tangy on her tongue, the sound of the sails when the wind shifted, and the rolling of the deck beneath her. When she blinked, the memory was gone, and it took a minute to understand Maire's words.

"A restaurant and gift shop." Maire tilted her head, her unfocused gaze on some point over AJ's right shoulder. "I think Sebastian would have been happy to know the monastery survived. And I do remember him mentioning something about cider, but I admit, I never paid close attention."

"They might not be following Sebastian's smuggling heritage, but they still include the local businesses in their ventures. Something of Sebastian survived." AJ glanced toward the back of the monastery where a chest-high wall had been added, blocking off her immediate view of the kitchen garden. "I wonder how many of the basement tunnels have been discovered. Or if the staircase down to the beach still exists."

Maire's shrug brushed against her shoulder. "I wonder what we'll be allowed to see. Will this Gallagher let us see the journal?"

She didn't want to admit to Maire she feared this visit wouldn't satisfy her questions. "I don't know, but we'll find out tomorrow."

"Maire, AJ," Ethan called. "Let's go. The others will wonder what happened to us."

AJ turned Maire back toward the car and noted Ethan's concerned expression. She nodded, and he left the professor to take AJ's place at Maire's side. He wrapped her in his arms, her head on his chest as they found their way to the car.

"Is Maire all right?" The professor strode next to AJ.

"She'll be fine. Just old memories."

"I see."

The professor didn't see at all. He could only guess because he wasn't ready to fully believe what the stones could do. And until he did, he could never fully appreciate the strong emotions this visit would revive. For the first time, AJ questioned their decision to spend the holidays here.

2

The next morning, AJ stretched like a feline before falling back into Finn's warm embrace. He grunted, still drowsy from their evening of lovemaking. He rolled into her, throwing an arm and leg over her as he nuzzled her neck.

"I'm glad you got over your shyness last night." He kissed her forehead.

AJ threw an arm over her eyes. "God. Don't remind me. I have to face her this morning."

"Her room is on the opposite side of the villa."

"I've never had sex in the same house where my mother was sleeping." Heat flamed her cheeks, and she pushed back, elbowing Finn when his lopsided grin teased her. "You'd understand if it were your mother."

He pulled her close. "Men don't think that way. Although, isn't Emory's room next to hers?"

She covered her face with her hands. "Stop. That's even worse."

He tugged her hands away and gave her a kiss that made her heart race and her toes curl. Then he swatted her backside and rolled away, quickly standing. "I can't believe how hungry I am."

AJ grinned. "You did have a bit of a workout last night."

His grin didn't falter as a lock of hair fell over his right eye. "Aye. And after breakfast, I'll be ready again."

She laughed. "I'm afraid that will have to wait. We have a monastery to tour."

"I remember a room or two in the basement where no one would find us."

She snorted, then turned serious. "Do you think they found all the secret rooms?"

He shrugged as he moved toward the bathroom. "It's been a long time. If Sebastian passed down the information to the younger monks, some of the rooms might have been discovered decades ago."

He leaned against the doorframe, and AJ couldn't help but gaze at his stunning physique and his ready smile, still amazed by how much he fought for her. What a lucky woman she was.

"We'll get a sense of who knows what while we're there. Until then..." He winked at her. "I think we have time to share a shower."

She was out of bed in a flash, and when he turned to enter the bathroom, she swatted his bare ass before pushing past him in a race for the shower.

After a busy breakfast of Adam's famous pancakes, all three cars departed from the villa with the same destination. The sun peeked out from the clouds with the promise of a better day. Helen and Madelyn would take the kids to the Cider House for a tour and play time in the updated stables while everyone else met with Gallagher before the monastery tour.

"Is Maire going to be okay?" Stella asked from the back seat as Finn drove into the parking lot. "She was rather quiet at breakfast."

"She's not sure what to expect. I'm not sure any of us are." AJ stuffed a bottle of water in her purse then pulled it back out. "Sebastian meant a great deal to us, helped us in so many ways, but he and Maire were quite close." AJ sidestepped her greatest fear—that Maire wanted to return to her normal time.

Finn grabbed her hand. "Maire hasn't quite found her place. If she were in her own timeline, she would probably have stayed at the monastery, becoming a student, and maybe one day settling down with a family. But being in the present, she's discovered more doors open to her knowledge and independence. She just needs time."

"We forced her hand in coming back with us. Maybe that was a mistake." AJ hated to admit it. Fortunately, Maire had acclimated well, and it helped that Ethan had months of time travel experience to guide her.

"She was in danger. Bringing her with us was the only answer. My sister can be melancholy at times. It started right after our parents' deaths. It's her way of working through the next steps. I think it's safe to say she'll be entirely focused on the monastery during our stay. But she needs this."

"Well, I say, whatever she needs to do to find her way, good for her." Stella pulled her purse to her and planted her face next to the window to get her first look at the monastery. "And a few pints of cider couldn't hurt."

AJ laughed. "Have we moved on from wine?"

"Oh, hell no. But when in Rome."

Finn shook his head and laughed as he parked the rental. He turned in his seat to face the two women. "Let's remember we're on vacation. Maire has a way of manipulating people to a cause. I would hope the two of you are aware of her ploys."

AJ and Stella glanced at each other, and they both nodded.

"No ploys, no games, no mischief." AJ crossed her chest, knowing it would do nothing to appease him.

"Absolutely. None of that." Stella winked at Finn before she stepped out of the vehicle.

"AJ." His tone sounded like he knew he'd already lost whatever battle might be coming.

She poked him in the stomach. "Don't worry." Then she kissed him. "It's not like bad guys are chasing us." She jumped out of the car before her own worry slipped past her well-guarded gates. Where Maire and the monastery was concerned —anything was possible.

"R emember, we're guests here." Ethan touched Maire's elbow, guiding her next to AJ and Finn who were a few steps ahead of them.

"I'm quite aware how to act in public." Maire's whispered words rushed out with a harsh tone, but Ethan wasn't troubled by them. He knew the reason behind her mood. Fear.

The last few months in Baywood had been good for Maire. He'd spent most of their time introducing her to new things—movies, libraries, cell phones, and new foods, ice cream being her favorite. They talked for hours most evenings, a fire blazing in the hearth while they stared out the tall windows to the dark ocean that lay behind their reflection. Yet, no matter how many topics they discussed, Maire purposely ignored conversation about the stones or the books. He watched her struggle when the conversation became close enough to bring the topic up, but she always steered the discussion to another subject. The business with the stones didn't feel complete. He understood that. There were too many questions left unanswered. But while he understood her concerns, he preferred to let the matter rest. The

Heart Stone was safe, and they needed to think about their future.

As he saw it, Maire hadn't discovered any pursuits that interested her. Ethan had restarted his security business, and while he maintained a small client base, it was enough to give him something to do. Maire had nothing but time to spend with AJ and Stella, but they had their own careers. Perhaps he should take another look at his and Maire's personal relationship. Maybe she didn't feel comfortable making a decision about her future because he hadn't given her a reason to. As independent as she was, she was still a woman from the eighteen hundreds. She would expect the man to make an offer if he was serious, no matter they were sleeping together. At the same time, he didn't want to pressure her into something so permanent when she hadn't voiced her own thoughts of the future.

He glanced at Finn and AJ. They had worked things out, but it hadn't been easy in the beginning. He should speak with one of them. Maybe both, but separately. Or better yet, Helen. She'd be more discreet.

Maire squeezed his hand. "Are you with us?"

He squeezed back. "I'm here. I'm feeling a bit scattered this morning." He put an arm around her. "I know how difficult this is for you. We have a few days, so take it slow."

If she was considering a response, it was lost in the introductions as Gallagher approached them just outside the outer courtyard. Gallagher appeared a bit scruffy with a full, graying beard and thinning hair that hung to his shoulders. His plaid shirt and cargo pants were already soiled, and if Ethan looked closer, he was sure to find lose dirt in the man's receding hairline.

"I thought we'd meet outside since it's shaping up to be a nice day." Gallagher carried a light Scottish accent, and the lines around his eyes reflected a cheery man. "And the tour will take us to some chilly places, so you'll want to make sure you're dressed appropriately." He glanced around and nodded, seemingly approving of their clothing. "Sorry for my appearance, but we found another chamber, and we've been digging our way in."

Maire and AJ glanced at each other but thankfully remained silent. It had to be difficult for them to not say something, They would know the tunnels better than anyone from the archaeological staff who had been here for the last year.

"We'll start the tour in the main building itself, then we'll go into the basement. The lower levels are closed, but after speaking to Professor Emory, we might be able to get you to one of the first sublevels. It will depend on where we are with clearing the other chamber."

He rubbed his hands together. "Any questions before we get started?"

Ethan held his breath and sighed when everyone shook their head.

"Instead of starting the tour through the side door, I thought we'd enter through the inner courtyard. It's the main entrance to the monastery and quite an amazing design." Gallagher continued his practiced spiel as he led them around the building to the large wooden doors that had been replaced at least once since Ethan had last been here.

As they walked, AJ and Maire huddled together, leaving Finn and Stella to walk together. Before they entered, Finn caught Ethan's gaze then nodded toward the two women. Ethan nodded in return. They would both watch over them. It was never a good sign when AJ and Maire were quiet. Only six months had passed since they'd last been here, and this particular entrance would be a difficult place to start.

Maire held onto AJ as they walked through the main doors into the inner courtyard. She felt AJ stiffen as she dragged Maire along, staying to the back of the group. Gallagher stopped in the center of the quiet yard and was explaining its purpose, which was large enough for carts to enter and turn around. This was where their group had entered the first time they met with the Duke of Dunsmore. She glanced up to the balcony. Only a few short months ago, she'd stood next to Sebastian on that balcony. Her knuckles had been white as she'd gripped her rifle, ready to shoot anyone attempting to leave. She smiled. Sebastian had secured the building and saved the monastery from Dugan's men.

"I can't believe how little has changed." AJ pulled her through the double doors that led to the foyer in the main building.

Maire had to agree. Somehow, the contractors had managed to get electricity in the building, and she assumed the wiring fit behind the walls that hid the stone beneath. That must be why the corridor felt narrow. But wall hangings still graced the hall. Some looked their age, but most, created in the same style, were newer.

"I love how they spruced everything up for the holidays." Stella's chipper voice sounded awed.

Maire took another look, not sure how she missed the garlands of holly and pine or the scent of cinnamon and cloves, at first thinking it must have floated in from the kitchen. But visions of gray walls, the dim glow of lanterns, and old tapestries flashed through her mind. She couldn't seem to reconcile the here and now from the past.

"Do you want to sit for a minute?" AJ asked. Her brow wrinkled and she squinted, something she'd begun doing before they ever boarded the airplane. She worried about her, and all

Maire could do was pat her arm; anything else would be useless.

"Everywhere I look I expect Sebastian to bustle around a corner or pop his head out of some secret passage."

"Remember the first time? I thought I'd pee myself." AJ laughed.

"I would have. The two of you were crazy brave with the duke's men just a few doors away." Stella had slowed so she could walk beside Maire.

Maire laughed at the idea of being brave. It had been a harrowing time, but all she remembered was the adrenaline. Her only thought at the time was for what they would discover. An incredible itch had built that wouldn't go away until she'd laid her hands on *The Book of Stones*. Now, that itch returned. Something was waiting for her here. She didn't know what, but she'd felt it as soon as Professor Emory suggested he join them on their trip. He hadn't said anything outright, but he had expectations. It might be something as simple as wanting to see his old friend's discovery. But Maire was certain, could feel it in her bones, that Gallagher had found something else. And she wouldn't leave until she knew what it was.

When the group began a more thorough tour, Maire begged off.

"Let's see if there's someplace by the kitchen we can wait. We can meet up with the tour before they go down to the basement." AJ began to move that way until Maire stopped her.

"No. I can't explain it, but I think you need to finish the tour."

AJ's brow lifted, and she stared at her. "What are you thinking?"

Maire shook her head. "I just need time to separate the time-lines. I wasn't expecting these feelings to be so strong."

Stella nodded. "I have that same feeling every spring when I can't remember which planter had the tulips and which one had the daffodils."

AJ rolled her eyes. "That's not the same thing."

But Maire couldn't help but chuckle. Stella balanced everything out, even with her unexpected comments, and it helped.

AJ got that look again, and Maire reached for her hand and gripped it tight, speaking low.

"As I said, I can't explain why, but I think it's important to know the layout of the place. See if anything has changed."

AJ pursed her lips. "When we get back to the villa, we're going to have a long talk." Then she glanced at Stella, who nodded. AJ wasn't going to leave without her having a babysitter.

"I'm quite good at talking my way into places." Stella took Maire's arm. "Why don't we see about a cup of tea to settle that stomach of yours."

Before she knew it, Stella was dragging her down the hallway as AJ turned to catch up with the group. Ethan had turned back to retrieve the wayward women, but when AJ reached him she turned him around while whispering something. He gave Maire a quick look, their eyes meeting briefly before they were pulled in opposite directions.

"Don't worry about them." Stella walked through the halls as if she'd been there before. "Let's see if I can find that monk I was talking to. But I think that scent of freshly baked bread will lead us straight to the kitchen."

3

———

AJ hurried back to the kitchen, not sure what to tell Maire. Gallagher had found a ledger, and all evidence pointed to it being Sebastian's. Same time period, similar handwriting. Worse, Gallagher wasn't interested in showing Sebastian's journal to anyone until after his team had thoroughly studied it. His team had over six months to inspect it, but supposedly just started a serious examination. She should wait for Ethan to tell Maire. Maybe they should wait until they got back to the villa. Some place private in case there was screaming involved.

She slowed as she approached the kitchen, reminding herself this was a different time, and the staff probably didn't take kindly to tourists wondering in. When she stuck her head through the door, she needn't have worried. If she hadn't been woolgathering on her way to the kitchen, she would have heard Stella's laugh from the halls.

The kitchen hadn't changed in all these years. The appliances were newer though appeared to be a couple decades behind what was currently available, but the large hearth was active with a toasty fire. The sturdy kitchen table appeared homemade and could seat a dozen. The door leading to the kitchen garden had been expanded to double doors, and the washing counters held deep sinks with added room for drying racks. Even with the modern upgrades, the kitchen was expansive, with plenty of room for a busy staff and spring harvests.

At the large table, Stella and Maire were surrounded by what appeared to be kitchen staff. They were all bent over whispering, the only interruption their laughter. AJ leaned against the doorframe, deciding whether to venture over or just watch for a while. Stella's voice rose above the others, but a deeper voice competed for attention. It came from a lean, older woman that, based on the rest of the heads at the table, was a good six inches taller than anyone else.

After a minute, AJ was drawn closer with a need to hear what everyone was gossiping about. She glanced around the kitchen but couldn't see anyone else. She'd only made it a few steps when a young boy brushed past her, heading straight for the table. He pushed his way onto the bench between two young girls at the end of the table, his attention square on the tall woman.

"AJ," Maire called. "You must join us. Sister Patrice has been telling us the history of the monastery."

The taller woman studied AJ, a gleam in her stern gaze that softened after her long perusal. "Yes, come sit." Sister Patrice elbowed the woman next to her, a much shorter and rounder woman, who looked about the same age. "Bea, put some more water on and get another cup for our Mrs. Murphy."

AJ was surprised the woman knew her name. The tour had taken an hour. If Stella and Maire had been here the entire time, the group could have covered a lot of topics.

"I think we learned more here than we could from a tour." Stella had a small flock of origami swans sitting in a corner and was making another. They had definitely been in the kitchen since they'd parted company. "Sebastian, who is a very well-known monk, has his own statue in the church. Did you know he was known for saving the monastery during the Terror? And it was his original idea to make cider. It took years before that came to pass, but it's been documented the idea came from him."

"He was quite influential, long after his death, at inspiring the Brotherhood to support themselves." Sister Patrice poured a cup of tea for AJ. "The prior listened and they found ways to work with the local village to trade for goods. This developed over time, helping the monastery survive the horrible wars that followed. Even after the events at Normandy, the monastery survived."

"If we can only survive the anarchists," Bea mumbled, and the younger girls giggled in response.

Patrice patted her hand and sighed. "The good Lord shall see us through this as well."

Maire smiled at AJ. "It appears Monsieur Gallagher and his crew aren't welcomed by all. His work has been stalled in several areas."

"Basically," Stella added, "he's been snooping into areas that weren't covered in the original agreement, which was to document the historical and archaeological significance of the monastery. The Brotherhood of Monks were quite specific on what and where the team could study. Obviously, with the age of the building, they could study this place for decades, but that would interrupt the monk's business and all their religious artifacts. Gallagher is trying to get the French Government to intercede on their behalf but seems they're unwilling to interfere with religious rights. It's all quite messy."

The others around the table nodded. A young woman brought over a large pot and refilled two smaller tea pots and added more tea leaves.

"It seems we came at a bad time." AJ sipped her tea, and for the briefest of moments, was mentally transported back to when she'd arrived at the monastery after leaving Beckworth tucked under a bush on a knoll. Sebastian had found her at Guerin's Inn. She'd never forget how relieved she'd been. Sebastian had sat her down at a similar table and plied her with tea and biscuits while she told him why she'd returned. He had been her neon light in the storm.

"No. This couldn't have been a better time." Patrice whispered something to one of the younger women, who scampered out the kitchen door. "Sorry, we need to get dinner started soon. But we want you to feel comfortable here. Maire mentioned you had ancestors who visited the monastery several times while Sebastian was here."

AJ choked on her tea and gave a quick glance to Maire, who simply nodded and avoided looking at her. Stella focused on her origami but wasn't fooling anyone while trying to hide a smile.

Patrice gave AJ another perusing study. "I believe it was a great, great, great, grandmother or grandfather?

AJ's stomach tightened and her mind raced. Why did the woman seem like she knew more than she did?

"Cook. I mean Sister Patrice, we could use Bea." A monk, maybe ten years older than AJ, stood near the door. "Brother Lucius is having trouble breathing again."

Patrice immediately nodded to Bea, who jumped up, rather spry for her age, and hustled to a cabinet. She retrieved a basket already filled to overflowing with bottles and vials, stuffed a few more in, then rushed over to follow the monk out.

"Brother Lucius is suffering from horrible winter chills. He's through the worst of it, but he still has congestion." Patrice began to gather the cups around her.

"Is there a hospital or clinic close?" AJ asked.

"Oh, oui. There's a very nice clinic in town, but we prefer natural remedies. There are times when we must call a doctor, but it is very rare." Patrice stood. "Please finish your tea. I would very much like to gather to speak again. Perhaps tomorrow after breakfast. Lunch is normally very simple here. A change from the old days, but with the cider press, the monks now prefer dinner for their larger meal."

"That would be wonderful." Maire stood and picked up cups, brushing away any assistance. "I'll just carry these to the sink."

When everyone left the table and returned to their kitchen duties, Stella leaned over to AJ. "I'm still not sure how someone as thin as Patrice could possibly be the head cook."

AJ laughed. "They probably don't fill themselves with pastries."

"And that's truly a shame."

When Maire returned, she elbowed AJ. "Finish up, we need to walk."

A J let Maire lead them through the halls of the monastery—special visitors were allowed to wander the first floor as long as they avoided the private rooms. She'd been the one to live within these halls during her weeks studying with Sebastian. Maire turned down a long hall that ran along the backside of the church. On the left, several doors led to rooms that also opened to the inner courtyard. These were the rooms where the duke's men had hidden in wait for them. A shiver ran down her back, remembering what she'd been told of the duplicity of Edward's men that had led to several deaths—including Edward's—as well as Finn's capture.

She walked with her head down, a band tightening her chest. At the end of the hall, a single door opened at the front of the monastery. The main entrance to the inner courtyard lay fifty feet to their left. AJ pushed her way out to the weak sunlight, then placed a hand on the wall as she took a deep, cleansing breath.

Maire stopped and, after glancing around, stared at the ground. "The path doesn't look like it's used very often."

"Is that a good thing?" Stella peered around Maire's shoulder.

A sinking feeling formed in the pit of AJ's stomach. "I don't think so, but let's follow it."

"I don't remember seeing the path from the road on the drive in," Maire called back without turning as she led the trio through scrub brush and damp earth, diverting around small puddles.

"I didn't look," She'd been too busy watching the road, still trying to remember it as nothing more than rock and dirt before it had been paved over. "I wonder the last time they used it. Maybe World War Two?"

"That would make sense based on what you've told me." Stella cursed after stepping in soft mud. "If Sebastian used it for smuggling, it would be a good place to hide things from the Germans."

"That's a long time to let the stairs go without maintenance with the salt air and blustery winters." AJ couldn't imagine what time would have done to wooden stairs.

Maire slowed, and AJ glanced around, searching for the connecting path that would lead in from the road. It was less recognizable than the path they were on, but they found it after making a few circles.

Maire turned right, then stopped. "Well, this is new."

AJ stepped in between Maire and Stella. The stairs were still there, but they weren't made of wood anymore. The wood had been replaced with iron. Her pulse raced. This was a good thing. Until she stepped closer. When Maire placed a foot on the first step, AJ pulled her back.

"I don't think we should trust these." She pointed to a lower step. "The salt air has corroded some of the iron. Since we don't know when the stairs were upgraded, it's hard to tell how sound they are."

She pushed and pulled on the stair railing and felt a bit of give. Not a good sign. She placed a foot on the first step and gave it her full weight. Then she bounced a bit and the staircase responded with a metallic creak. It would probably hold one person, if they stepped carefully. But all three of them? Maybe one at a time.

Maire pulled her back. "Let's follow it as far as we can and see what it looks like farther down."

They were able to glimpse another fifteen feet from where they stood before the stairs dropped away as they followed the cliff toward a landing before continuing down to the bay. The landing was nothing more than a bedroom-sized, rocky ledge that led to the iron door.

"We'll have to crawl out to the edge to see any more, but did you see that one bolt, just before the steps disappeared? It looked a bit hinky to me." Stella stepped closer, but AJ pulled her back.

"It's something to consider." She glanced at Maire. AJ had been through various emotional times with her—joy, fear, anger, and certainly disappointment. And it was the latter that was clearly stamped on her friend's face.

AJ studied the ground. No one was willing to lay on the damp earth. Not in what they were wearing. The mud would be difficult to explain and would end up in the rental car. She put an arm around Maire's shoulder. "Let's not give up hope until we've checked the iron door."

She led the way this time, moving away from the stairs and down a non-existent path, but one AJ easily remembered. It had only been a few months after all. She stopped at another edge and squatted. Maire and Stella followed suit.

"The iron door." Stella rubbed her arms. "After listening to all the stories and then walking through the monastery, somehow, this door is what makes it all real."

"They added a padlock." Just one more thing not in their favor. AJ couldn't believe the bad luck, but what had she expected after all this time?

"Do you think they need two keys? One for the padlock and one for the door itself?" Maire's tone sounded discouraged, and AJ wasn't sure how to respond that wouldn't completely crush her hopes.

"My best guess is that they either don't want to chance losing their only key for the door, or it was lost long ago. The padlock is probably the only thing keeping the door locked."

"It's strange they would lock it from the outside. Wouldn't that mean the stairs are viable?" Maire's voice took an upbeat tone.

AJ couldn't argue the point. "But who knows when that padlock was put on. I need my binoculars. We could get a better look at the lock, but still, we would need a key."

Stella snorted. "I can pick it if we can't find the key."

Maire and AJ turned as one to stare at Stella. It took Stella a moment while she squinted down at the padlock before she noticed the two staring at her.

"What? So, I was a bit more unscrupulous when I started out. I learned to pick locks to get into places. I'm nosy. That shouldn't be news." She hesitated. "I might want to practice, just to get the kinks out."

Maire rolled her eyes, and AJ laughed. Her two best friends. Stella could still surprise her after all this time. And Maire had picked up the unfortunate habit of rolling her eyes. Would she start the trend when she returned home? AJ froze. What made her think that? But she knew. The feeling never completely went away since they'd returned from their last jump. As much as

Maire had begun to fit in, there was always a sense she'd go home. Her thirst for more knowledge of the stones was unquenchable. And it broke AJ's heart to know Maire had to do whatever was needed to satisfy that thirst.

She wiped her eyes and stood. "Let's get back. I want to see the stairs from below if I can. Otherwise, the only way in will be through the monastery if we can't find a way to make these stairs safer."

"Which isn't completely out of the question." Maire scratched her cheek. "We made friends today. Friends who are disgruntled with these archaeologists. We could find someone who can get us to the sublevels and might also know the history of the stairs."

AJ nodded. "Let's not completely write off Emory. Gallagher suggested a private meeting tomorrow afternoon to discuss Sebastian's journal and another ledger he found."

"You're just telling me now?" Maire's eyes narrowed.

Stella nodded. "Seems like that should have been the first thing you mentioned. You're starting to sound like me." She was apparently in solidarity with Maire.

AJ rubbed her forehead. "I know. I was just surprised by you swapping stories with the kitchen staff. Then all the talk about checking the entrances to the sublevels. It kind of seemed like the wrong time to bring it up."

Maire sat, her backside hitting hard, but she didn't seem to notice. "Did he say what the ledger was?" Her voice was low, and AJ could kick herself for bringing this up now.

AJ sat with her, and Stella followed. The three sat in a triangle, their heads bent together like children with a secret, the soft dirt underneath them forgotten.

"Not really, but it sounded like it might have belonged to Sebastian. But why Gallagher referred to it as a ledger rather than another journal, I can't say."

Silence followed, and as it stretched, Maire gave AJ a solemn look.

"What is it?" AJ's stomach clenched, not sure she was going to like what was coming next. Stella wouldn't meet her eyes.

"Before you found us in the kitchen," Maire paused and released a shaky breath. "Patrice told us there were no records of Sebastian's death. They don't know when he died or where he's buried."

AJ was stunned. "How could that be? With his statue and how much he's meant to the monastery." She paused. Had he wandered off and never returned home? Sebastian was a smart man, very adept at reading the books and knowing how time travel worked. Maybe he jumped to another time. Then it came to her. "He did that on purpose."

Maire and Stella stared at her.

"Why would he do that?" Maire's words were filled with pain, or maybe she was hurt that he would die without a trace.

"When you were kidnapped the second time, I told Sebastian that Ethan had come to the future in a wild attempt to find a clue from history that might tell us where you'd gone." She laughed. "It was Gallagher who'd found the journal where Sebastian had written about the note he'd received from Elizabeth Ratliff. She told him her father had gone to Waverly to visit the viscount and had been killed by highwaymen. That was why we thought Beckworth had been jumping to the past. We hadn't known about Reginald."

Maire ran a finger through the damp earth, making circles. "I went to the future, and he didn't want me to discover how and when he died in case I returned before his death."

"If it were me, I'm not sure I'd want to go back and know when and how my friend would die." Stella shivered. "And then there are all those questions. Should you tell them? Should you try to stop it? You know, if it wasn't a natural death."

"I hadn't even considered that." When Maire released her breath this time, she was smiling. "Somehow that makes me feel better."

The three quieted again, and AJ turned her gaze to the bay, her thoughts turning back to their current predicament. "As much as Gallagher wants to protect Sebastian's journal, he's been helpful to us in the past."

"I wonder what's so interesting in this ledger he found." Stella had found a twig and was connecting Maire's circles in the dirt with squiggly lines.

AJ snorted. "Sebastian had been running illicit cargo through the monastery. Maybe the ledger is a record of those transactions."

Maire smiled. "He always had a rebellious streak. I wonder what his admirers would say to know their hero was a smuggler."

"They'd love him even more." Stella's comment was said with such conviction, the other two could only stare. "What?" She shook her head. "Honestly, why am I the only one that notices these things? Everyone loves and admires Sebastian, but not just for saving the monastery and his compassion for others. They love that he worked with the town, that he took it as his responsibility to keep everyone safe. The fact that he did it under everyone's noses, and that he was just like everyone else? Someone who took an advantage and turned it into a risk for survival? I bet a year from now, he'll have a larger statue." She tipped her head to the side. "Maybe a second statue in the middle of the outer courtyard."

Maire sniffled, then wiped her nose. "Of course, he was a man who survived the Revolution and the Terror. Smugglers were heroes to the common man." She clapped her hands, her signal of a change in topic. "What time is this meeting with Gallagher? We have a meeting with Patrice before lunch. We need to keep to that. But I want to see Sebastian's journal, regardless of what this ledger is."

"That should be easy enough." Stella leaned back on her hands and glanced up at the gray clouds being chased away by the sun.

"I'm not so sure," AJ responded. "The journal will be considered an historical document. What we learned in the kitchen about the hostility between the two groups brings back something Gallagher said earlier today. There seems to be an issue about who owns the journal. Right now, it's in Gallagher's hands so he's keeping it under tight control, kind of like the rule of possession along with his claim of protecting it."

"I'm not leaving until I see that journal." Maire folded her arms across her chest.

AJ inwardly sighed, having already suspected that would be Maire's stance. "I agree that Sister Patrice is our best option. We should try to meet more of the staff if we can. Then we'll see what Gallagher has, and what he's willing to offer."

4

Children squealed as they raced through the kitchen then through the dining room, running around the table, two grown men—Finn and Ethan—chasing after them.

"Argh, fair game for our pirate stew." Finn's pirate voice sounded a little too real, and AJ wondered, not for the first time, how Finn made his fortune while time traveling around the States with the *Daphne*.

"I say we make them walk the plank and feed them to the fishes," Ethan bellowed. He held up his left hand, which he shaped into the form of a hook.

Charlotte giggled so much she began to hiccup.

"All right, children." Helen clapped her hands and left no room for doubt that Finn and Ethan somehow fit into the same category as the other kids. "It's time for baths, and if you're good, we'll read you a fitting pirate story before bed."

"Yes!" Patrick pumped his skinny arm before grabbing Robbie by a shoulder and pushing him toward the hall that led to their rooms. Charlotte raced behind them, her feet doing double time to her brother's longer strides, her hiccups echoing in the hall, and Helen right on their heels.

Finn laughed as he pulled two beers from the fridge, handing one to Ethan before falling into a chair. "How do you keep up with those three every day?"

"Mostly we don't," Adam said from the patio. He scrubbed the grill then closed the lid. He'd cooked steaks for dinner and their group ate every morsel. The table had been cleared of everything but wine, beer, and a handful of napkins.

Stella kept the napkins close. She was teaching Charlotte origami and needed to build up her practice stash.

Adam walked in and placed the grill utensils on the kitchen counter. He grabbed a beer for himself but topped off the women's wine glasses before sitting next to the professor. "When Patrick was born, Madelyn and I read all the books and followed all the recommendations. Wore us down to babbling idiots. When Robbie came along, we quickly learned the difference between an urgent scream and screams between brothers. Charlotte's early illness aside, it's a wonder she survived the early years. Now they're just little hellions. We figured it best to wait until they got older before laying down any strict rules. We can take them out in public without too many problems, and they behave in school. We call it good enough."

"What they really mean," AJ chipped in, "is that Mom has been instrumental in their education and proper social behavior."

Adam lifted his beer. "Here, here!"

They all laughed. Even Maire, who had been quiet throughout dinner as Professor Emory and the men discussed the the tour of the monastery, could find humor in the discussion. Fortunately, Maire held her tongue throughout dinner as she'd promised. And though she appeared interested in the multitude of topics, AJ wasn't fooled. The woman had the patience of a cat on a hunt and was just waiting for her moment to pounce.

Professor Emory, who was still sitting at the head of the

table, clasped his hands over his stomach. "I must say. This has been one of the best days I can remember."

"We didn't get a chance to thank Gallagher for giving us a personal tour." Adam pushed back his chair so he could rest a leg over a knee.

"I'm sorry he seemed so distracted." The professor shook his head, pushed his glasses up his nose, and took a sip of tea.

"He seemed fine to me." Stella placed a paper fish on the table and went to work on another one. She'd always dabbled in other shapes besides swans, but with Charlotte's interest, she seemed to have become more motivated to attempt other figures.

"Oh, if you knew him for as long as I have, you would have noticed his mind was someplace else. He's probably given so many tours he can do them blindfolded."

"He was still generous with his time, and we appreciate it." Ethan glanced at Maire, and he squeezed her hand. If she noticed, she didn't respond, her focus square on the professor.

AJ was surprised, and grateful, Maire had the control to not mention the journal yet.

Emory nodded. "Well, I can't say for sure, but I think this ledger he discovered has his full attention. He can't seem to talk of anything else."

"Did they determine who the ledger belonged to?" Stella was either playing straight man or had an interest of her own. History wasn't typically Stella's thing, but from what Adam had shared, she'd become interested in the stones since the first time she met Emory. Partly because she was smitten with the older man, like a student with a favorite teacher.

"They're not positive, but based on paper and ink analysis it seems to be the same era as the monk's ledger. Gallagher is convinced it's the same handwriting." Emory's eyes sparkled, and he rubbed his hands together. "What I'd give to see what else is down in the tunnels."

AJ glanced at Maire and was sorry she did. Maire's eyes were round with silent pleading. She understood her friend's reasoning. If Maire brought up the question of the journal, Ethan and Finn would worry she was becoming obsessed. Again. And to be honest, AJ would have to agree with them. At the same time, she understood Maire's need to learn all she could. She missed Sebastian, and this was the closest she could get to him in this timeline. The things AJ did for friends.

"So, Professor, do you think Gallagher would let us see Sebastian's journal?" AJ gave him an innocent if not eager expression. Or she hoped that was how her smile would come across.

"Quite doubtful, I would think. It's stored in a special airtight case. Only specially trained interns are allowed to handle it. Though he's been considering separating the pages out of the journal so they could be displayed individually. He has the interest of a couple museums."

This wasn't good. Maire sat rigid and her hands gripped the arms of the chair.

"They're taking the journal out of the monastery?" Stella's brows had lifted, and she'd dropped the figure she was making.

The professor scratched his head and pushed his spectacles up. "That's a tricky question right now. The monks consider it their property. They claim they only gave the archaeological society permission to study the area, not remove anything. But Gallagher believes the journal is of historical significance, and the society has a request, which is currently in front of a judge, to remove the journal and a few other artifacts."

"Do they have any legal support?" Adam asked.

The professor shrugged. "With the current political climate, I think Gallagher has a tough sell. Taking something that was clearly personal notes from one of the monks, regardless of how long ago it was, would be seen as trampling on the monks' rights to what they see as belonging to their brotherhood."

AJ sighed heavily. One problem averted for now.

"Do you think Gallagher could be persuaded to show us one page?" Ethan held up a hand, although no one was stopping him from asking questions. "I think you know how important it is for the ladies to understand something more about their heritage."

A solid point to Ethan for remembering their cover story. AJ had been caught off guard and could have kicked herself when Maire mentioned their non-existent ancestors to Patrice.

"I guess I could ask him tomorrow, but that does bring up another point Gallagher shared with me. It seems they don't have the entire journal."

"What?" Maire gasped. Ethan moved closer, maybe thinking this would be the time she came unglued and did something regretful. AJ shifted to the edge of her seat, just in case.

"I don't know why he wouldn't have known that right off, but now that they've had more time to study it, they believe they only have the first half. It's unknown if the other pages survived." Emory leaned back when Helen brought over a fresh cup of tea. "He also mentioned little side notes on each page that appear to be some form of code."

Maire sat up and pushed Ethan's hand away. "Professor Emory. You've been very kind in introducing us to your friend. I understand how fragile the journal must be after all this time. It certainly helped that it had been stored in cooler conditions, and he's correct that the journal should be kept in a case unless being actively studied." She paused, then rubbed her hands along her slacks as if pressing out a wrinkle. "Would it be possible to just look at it in its case? Do you know if they stored it with the journal closed or with the pages opened?"

Emory tapped his chin. "I don't remember him mentioning

it, but I would think they would leave the pages open so they could easily refer to the writing. That would minimize how often they had to touch it." He held Maire's gaze then gave her a gentle smile. "I can't see what harm that could do. I believe one of the monks was also requesting a look at it. Perhaps a show of good faith with the monks and their friends would help Gallagher's case."

Maire beamed and her features relaxed. Then she gulped a long swallow of wine.

AJ glanced at the others. No one believed anything would help Gallagher's case where the monk's property was concerned, but if it got them a view of the journal, no one would question it.

J stared out at the dark sea, her focus on a bobbing light on some distant ship. The days spent on the *Daphne* flooded her. The storm when they crossed the Irish Sea was the first that popped in her head. She'd been so lost at the time, yet it was one of her best memories. But there had been many on that ship. As much as she missed the *Daphne*, Finn must miss her ten times over.

His arm moved around her waist, bringing her closer. The scent of cedar wrapped around her, and she leaned into him, his chin resting on her head. She grabbed on to his arm and blinked away tears. Maybe it hadn't been a good idea coming here so soon. The memories had barely been laid to rest and here they were digging them all up again.

"I feel it, too. The sense of loss." He wrapped his other arm around her and hugged her. "I don't think time will ever fade what we we've been through. A tall ship at sea, the monastery, the robust aroma of arriving in Portishead."

She laughed. "My god, that was the worst smell ever. Even as horrid as the stink was in the back streets of London, nothing could compare to my first landing in England."

He kissed her temple, and she sensed his grin. "What would have happened had we never left Ireland?"

"We'd have either killed each other within another year or starved to death in the potato famine."

"Well, now, that's a cheery thought."

She turned in his arms. "Fortunately, we're both too stubborn to let fate guide our hand."

He kissed her, his lips gentle and undemanding. "No. Just the fog."

She snorted. "We don't seem to know when to walk away."

"Which turned out to be the right thing." He turned her toward a chair. "Come. We haven't had much time to ourselves lately."

Once she was seated, he handed her a cup. He'd made hot chocolate, and a touch of cinnamon tickled her nose. Her mother's recipe. They sat in comfortable silence, staring out the window. Something they'd done dozens of times at home, and her earlier tumultuous contemplations evaporated, leaving her languid.

"Where did you and Ethan disappear to after the tour?"

"To town. We were both interested in seeing if Guerin's Inn had survived."

"And?"

"Aye, it's still there. Neither of us could believe it. His ancestors still own it. Underneath all the new beer taps, music, and a fresh coat of paint, the rest hasn't changed much. The large hearth is still there and was roaring when we arrived for lunch and an ale. They still have rooms upstairs, but I don't know if they rent any of them."

"That would have taken some work to update."

"Do you want to run away and a spend a night there?" He

glanced at her over his mug of cocoa, his brows wriggling with invitation.

She laughed. "I think I'll leave those memories as is. As much as I'm sure they have upgraded their beds, the one here suits me just fine." She reached over with her stocking foot and rubbed her toes along his leg. "The docks must be different."

"Oh, aye, there's a full marina there now, though I doubt it sees anything as large as the tall ships anymore. The docks were filled with fishing boats and pleasure crafts."

"We should plan a day there. Something tells me we'll need to get Maire away from the monastery for a while."

"How bad is it?"

She shrugged. "Not much more than you'd expect coming back here. But knowing Sebastian's journal is within arm's reach, she won't be satisfied until she's at least seen it."

"Is that all? You spent almost all day there."

AJ set her cup down. "Maire and Stella made friends with the kitchen staff, and we spent time listening to stories of the monastery. Then we wandered around the building and court-yard, sharing more stories with Stella." She stood and held out her hand. "Enough about our day. I'm more interested in the rest of our evening."

He took her hand. She'd barely taken a step before he lifted her in his arms to the sound of her giggles. "You're not trying to distract me, are you?" He gave her a sound kiss before tossing her on the bed.

"This brings back memories." She removed her sweater, wiggled out of her leggings, then tossed her socks and bra across the room. She delighted every time his eyes darkened. Her nerves tingled and heat blossomed through her as she watched him undress.

When he removed the last stitch, she almost drooled at the sight. His muscular frame, that lopsided grin, and the love in his eyes turned the heat growing in her to boiling. He took a step closer. "I remember the first time you waited for me with that gleam in your eyes. God, I can still feel the roll of the *Daphne* against the timid waves as the anticipation filled me. Just seeing your desire, the love you have for me..." He paused, "I can't believe what a lucky man I am."

"We might not have the ship, but come a little closer, and I promise to rock your world."

He was on her in a heartbeat, tucking her beneath him as his mouth streamed butterfly kisses down her neck and over her breasts. Goosebumps rose as his fingers danced lightly over her skin, moving down her belly, forcing her body to arch against him with fierce need.

Before he entered her, he kissed her and whispered in her ear. "You rock my world every morning you wake by my side and every evening you fall asleep in my arms. We're forever, you and I."

And though it wasn't possible, AJ felt the sway of the *Daphne* as Finn took her breath away.

5

Gallagher's first floor office used to be the creamery, but since the monastery no longer owned cows, they purchased milk from a local dairy and made cheese in another room. Maire had lived at the monastery when she'd first met Sebastian and walked to the room every morning for fresh cream. The room seemed smaller than she remembered, but now bookshelves lined the walls, and a long table filled the center of the room where everyone waited. Gallagher was late from another meeting that Professor Emory had been invited to join.

Adam and Stella sat across from Maire, Ethan and AJ on either side of her. Madelyn had taken the children to town, so Finn stayed behind to keep Helen company. They'd also decided Gallagher might be more receptive to their request if the women negotiated with him. And if necessary, the professor agreed to support them.

Maire rubbed her hands on her slacks. The journal called to her. It was so close. A quick walk down the hall to the stairs leading to Sebastian's hideaway—his library. Ethan rested a hand on hers, then grasped it.

"It will be all right." His words were soft and earnest. "Surely, he won't see a problem with you just looking at it through the case."

She wasn't so sure, but she squeezed his hand then brought it up and kissed his knuckles before rubbing them against her cheek. When the door opened, she took a deep breath, released Ethan's hand, and gathered herself for battle.

Professor Emory followed Gallagher into the room. The professor gave everyone a tired smile before lowering his head and taking a seat. Maire's heart sank. Gallagher stood, his chest puffed out, his thin hair pulled back in a ponytail. His plaid shirt was cleaner than the last time she'd seen him. She smirked. It must have been cleaning day. Then she chided herself for uncharitable thoughts. As Stella would remind her, karma was a bitch, and she was already treading on thin ice where this man was concerned.

She turned on her brightest smile and greeted Gallagher with as much politeness as the others.

"Sorry to keep you all waiting. We had a conference call with the French Historical Society to bring them up to speed on the ledger we found." He wiped his brow even though it was chilly in the room. "Professor Emory said you had some additional questions after our tour yesterday."

"Thank you for sharing your valuable time with us." AJ took the lead as they had planned.

"Not at all. We enjoy visitors from America, and I know since my discussions with the professor earlier in the year that you had an interest in the stones we discovered." He scratched his beard. "I believe you mentioned yesterday that your ancestors had visited the monastery during the Terror?"

"Actually, it was during the Napoleonic Wars. They visited twice. Once in 1802 and again in 1804."

"Ah, they were here after the war started again. How did they get into France? It would have been difficult during those times."

AJ hesitated, then glanced at Ethan. They hadn't planned to discuss their foray into the monastery.

"Smugglers." Ethan never paused and said it with a grin to match Gallagher's.

"Smugglers? Really?" Gallagher took a seat and scratched his beard again. It was either an affectation or the man had something growing in it.

A knock at the door interrupted the discussion. It opened slowly and an older man, about the same age as Sebastian when she'd last seen him, lumbered in. He was a robust man of average height and walked with a slight limp. His hair was a blending of blond and gray that was pleasing against his leathery, tanned skin. He coughed then wiped his mouth with a handkerchief he kept balled up in his left hand.

Gallagher began to get up until the old man waved him off. "Brother Lucius. Should you be up?"

The three women glanced at each other. Patrice had mentioned the man yesterday and given the impression the man was bed-ridden. But when Maire thought back to the conversation, Patrice had said he was on the mend except for a cough.

"I'm fine." Lucius coughed into his handkerchief again. "The exertion makes me cough more but Bea's tea..." He gave a jolly laugh. "I just love saying that, but Bea's tea worked wonders. I'll need another day or two before venturing out to the gardens, but I'm not too old or sick to hobble around the monastery." He glanced around the table. "Hello, everyone, and pardon my interruption. Continue on, we can do introductions later." He pinned his gaze on Maire before turning to AJ. "Did I hear something about smugglers?"

"Yes." AJ sat up, deciding to run with Ethan's opening. "It seems my ancestor was a bit of a rogue." She gave Gallagher a conspiratorial smile and wink. Then she scooted closer to the table and lowered her head as if she had more secrets to share.

Gallagher and Lucius both leaned in as if drawn by puppet strings.

"He owned a ship and ran cargo between England and Ireland. But when the war broke out, he turned his eyes to France." She sat back, having Gallagher's full attention.

Maire swallowed her own grin when AJ began to spin a yarn that spoke of Finn rather than some make-believe relative.

"We're not sure how he found his way to the monastery. Based on what little we could find in old diaries, we suspect he started by occasionally running cargo for the duke while England and France were still at peace."

"That would have been the 1802 visit." Gallagher nodded. "We found evidence of an English duke at the monastery during that time, but there are very few details."

"Our best guess," AJ continued, "was that my ancestor must have heard of Brother Sebastian's smuggling operation from other ship's captains while docked in town."

"Are you saying Brother Sebastian was a smuggler?" Gallagher's wide-eyed expression told everyone what they suspected. The man hadn't put two and two together with the ledger yet.

Brother Lucius laughed and slapped a hand on the table. "That old goat. We had a feeling there was more to Sebastian's saving of the monastery." He turned his gaze on Gallagher. "I haven't had time to view the ledger you found, but I suspect it could be the inventory of his operations."

Gallagher paled. "We need to run additional tests to validate the radiocarbon analysis. Perhaps in a few weeks..."

"Nonsense." The monk's booming voice was clear and strong, and Maire waited for a cough that didn't materialize. "My understanding of the decree, although informal, was that all objects discovered within the monastery and surrounding buildings would be shared with me or the prior within twenty-four hours."

Gallagher swallowed hard and then scratched his beard. "Yes, I'm sorry, but when you got sick, we thought we'd have time to prepare the document." Maire wasn't sure she believed him. It was more likely he'd hoped no one else at the monastery had been told about the decree.

Brother Lucius nodded. "Yes, I see. And with the prior out of the country, that would make sense. But I'm back to work now." He glanced at AJ before turning a soft gaze on Maire. "I would think while you're showing me the ledger, it would be a good time to let these good people get a look at Sebastian's journal."

Gallagher sat up as though someone had ruffled his feathers. "That is entirely inappropriate. The document is too fragile..."

With a wave of his hand, Brother Lucius silenced Gallagher. "Nonsense. The journal has been enclosed in a glass case for weeks. They only want to see it. And, quite frankly, since the monastery claims ownership over the journal, we see no reason not to grant access."

Professor Emory cleared this throat. "Gallagher, I believe you were going to tell us what you discovered in the ledger. I'm sure everyone would be interested in hearing about it."

"Good God, I thought I might've had to slit my throat." Stella dropped into a chair on the patio at the Cider House.

AJ fell in next to her. She couldn't argue, her mind was numb, but she was too exhausted from boredom to respond.

"I have to admit I'd heard enough after fifteen minutes, and I remember moving some of that inventory for Sebastian." Ethan poured cider from a pitcher while Maire set down two plates of appetizers.

"Now that I'm here, seeing all this firsthand, I have to say that statement just doesn't sit right with me. The reality of you being here, in this place, two hundred years ago?" Adam shook his head as he grabbed a small plate and began moving appetizers to it. "I usually enjoy details, but how many barrels of whiskey or bolts of fabric do we need to hear about?"

"Damascus silk," Maire said.

"Oh, yes. That makes all the difference." Adam took a long swig of ale, ignoring Maire's return glare.

"I think we could all use something to eat." Ethan passed around the plates, giving AJ a pleading look.

"And a shit load to drink." Stella lifted her mug then took a tentative sip. Then a longer one. "That's pretty good stuff. And fairly potent."

"Their bitter apple cider is one of the top ten ciders in the country," Adam said.

"Did you learn that on the tour?" AJ licked her lips after setting down her mug. She had to admit the cider would compete well against some of the Oregon cidermakers.

Adam nodded. "They mentioned it on the tour, but I'd already read it on the flight over."

"Of course, you did." Stella stuffed cheese wrapped in something AJ didn't recognize into her mouth.

"Do you think someone coached Brother Lucius into supporting our efforts?" Maire asked. She bit the end of a cracker, her gaze unfocused as she stared at the monastery.

AJ had been thinking the same thing, especially after the monk had given her and Maire long looks. She shivered. It was like he could read their thoughts.

"His response seemed too much on the nose for not knowing something," Ethan, always the logical one. "But I don't remember his name coming up in the tour or discussions with Emory."

"Sister Patrice." Maire sat up. "It had to be. Who else?"

"Or maybe Bea." Stella glanced around when everyone looked at her. "What? She left the kitchen to take him herbs of some sort yesterday."

"I forgot about that." Maire pulled at her lip. "She might have mentioned our story as something to pass the time while mixing the herbs. Or Patrice asked her to say something."

"That makes more sense. He acts like he knows things we haven't shared." AJ sat back, pulled a leg up and wrapped an arm around it. Maire and Stella had been right about getting to know the staff. It had worked so many other times, she didn't know why she hadn't thought of it herself. But she was still reminiscing, or rather, falling back into time whenever a memory slammed into her.

"Maybe he saw it as an opportunity to push the monk's stance on who owns the artifacts," Adam said.

"That's a stronger possibility." Ethan smiled at Maire. "But as long as it got us in, I'm not going to question it."

AJ squinted into the distance. A man strode over from the parking lot, heading directly toward them. She'd know that self-assured swagger anywhere. What was Finn doing here? Not that she was complaining. Any opportunity to watch him never disappointed.

"How did your meeting go? Are you celebrating or drowning your sorrows?" Finn's grin was wide, and he winked at AJ before leaning down to give her a light kiss that warmed her heart.

"Celebrating. I had it as a fifty-fifty shot, but it seems we have friends at the monastery." Stella's comment lifted Finn's brow.

"We can discuss it over dinner. I'd like to hear Emory's thoughts." Adam finished his cider.

"Do you have time for a drink?" Ethan offered the pitcher to Finn.

Finn checked his watch. "No. I'll wait."

Ethan finished his mug, stood, and handed the car key to AJ.

"Where are you going?" AJ took the key but focused on Finn.

"We have a date with some locals and a dart board." Finn held his grin in place. "Would you like to come with?"

AJ studied him. "No. We have a meeting with Patrice this afternoon. And we might hear more why Brother Lucius helped us."

"Excellent idea." Adam stood. "Do you think you could drop me by the villa on the way to town?"

"Absolutely." Finn clapped Adam on the shoulder.

Ethan gave Maire a quick kiss. "We'll see you back at the villa. Stay out of trouble if possible. At least until after you see the journal."

Maire swatted him, and the three women watched the men walk away.

"He's up to something." AJ kept her eye on the men until they disappeared behind the cars in the lot.

Stella turned around in her seat. "He seemed normal to me."

AJ glanced at Maire, who shrugged. "Maybe. I admit I haven't been paying attention to much more than the journal."

AJ let it go—for now. Something was off, but unable to decipher any clues or pin down any specifics, she turned her attention back to Stella and Maire. They had their own secrets.

"O kay, we have a solid two-hour window, but I wouldn't push us past that." Adam slammed the car door and stretched out in the back seat.

Finn glanced at Adam through the rearview mirror then put the car in drive. "I'd hoped for three." There was a lot to do in the next few days. He may have overestimated how long the monastery would occupy the women's time.

"Do you think AJ suspects something?" Ethan turned around

from the front seat so he could more easily speak with both men.

Finn rubbed his jaw. He thought he was the only one that noticed. There wasn't any reason for her to be suspicious of anything. It was those damn reporter instincts of hers. She might smell something amiss, but she wouldn't have anything but suspicions. "I'll keep her busy." He ignored their stares. "So where first?"

"Reviewing the plan, it looks like we should start at the marina and get that out of the way." Ethan ran a finger down a piece of paper he'd pulled out of his pocket. "I think the rest of this list is in a decent order, so I say we just follow it."

"Good. That's settled." Adam gazed out the window. "I put that list in the order I thought we should tackle it."

"The marina it is." Finn drummed his fingers on the steering wheel. "How did you get Gallagher to let us see the journal?"

"It wasn't us," Adam kept his focus on the window, or perhaps what lay beyond.

Ethan gave Finn a recap on the meeting. "So, we're not sure what his motives were, but Brother Lucius laid down a gauntlet on the ownership of the journal. Whether that remains to be true after the court hearing, we'll be long gone."

"So, we take advantage while we can." Finn liked the thought of that. That was how things were done in 1804 and times before. And humanity hadn't changed in all that time. "Do we know anything about Brother Lucius?"

That broke Adam's daydreaming. He pulled his phone out and started typing. "Let's see what I can find."

"In the meantime," Ethan broke in, "I think Adam should spend as much time with his family as he can. You and I can keep an eye on the women."

Finn nodded. "We can use the time they spend together."

"I should be able to take care of number five on the list when

KIM ALLRED

I take Madelyn and the kids on a farm tour tomorrow." Adam tucked his phone away. "I'll need to spend some quiet time researching the monk. I'll do it when I get back to the villa."

Finn pulled into the marina's lot and parked so the car faced the boats. He missed the *Daphne II*. Once they got home, he'd take AJ on a city hop down the West Coast. Just the two of them on the boat, making their own memories on the new *Daphne*.

Ethan slapped his arm. "Come on. It's time to relive some old haunts."

6

Stella plopped into a chair at the Cider House and wrapped her jacket around her. The weak winter sun was losing its battle with the clouds and did nothing to combat the chill of the breeze. At least the patio had heaters, though they were positioned too far away in her opinion.

AJ set two mugs of cider on the table, then dragged a heater closer to their table. "I probably shouldn't do that, but most people are sitting inside."

Stella glanced around. "I hadn't noticed. After all that time sitting in one room, I needed some air."

"I don't mind. I needed a break."

"This is twice in one day that we've been here. They're going to think we're moving in."

After several minutes, AJ sighed.

Stella knew that sound. "Tell me what you're thinking."

AJ shook her head. "It's just strange. Sitting here and looking at the outer courtyard. So much seems the same, like the old cobblestones and the rock wall. Our first time in France, when Finn had been captured by the duke and his men, the *Daphne Marie* had sailed along the coast lobbing cannon at the cliff as a distraction. The rock wall was all but demolished, as was part of this courtyard." She turned around to glance at the building where the cider mill resided. "Luckily they missed the stables." She settled back in her chair and sipped her drink. "This really is good cider." She used a napkin to wipe her lips.

"If I remember the story Finn told, you were the one to talk someone into doing that. Who was it? Jamie. Was he the captain?"

AJ shook her head. "Finn was still captain then. Jamie was his second mate, though he was rather young for the role. Lando had taken over as first mate." She laughed. "It was all rather confusing at the time."

"I'm surprised at how little you said has changed in all this time."

AJ plucked at her sweater. "Monks aren't into aesthetics or showing wealth. I think they only did this—" she twirled her hand to encompass the cider mill and patio, "—to make it more pleasing for their customers. In truth, it seems the stable was the only building to get a major upgrade after all these centuries. Everything else has been done to keep the old building viable."

Stella studied AJ. She'd seen both her and Maire fall in and out of moods since their arrival. She had no idea what to say or do, feeling like an outsider to everything that had happened here. Finn seemed the only one who didn't seem to be bothered by the return. Even Ethan turned quiet at times, but that might be his reaction to Maire's mercurial swings. But most men knew how to hide their emotions.

Still, she was glad to be here, to experience as much as she could of AJ's journey. One thing was certain. Stella had no fancy whims. She would never have survived as well as AJ had.

"I don't think I ever told you." AJ rubbed a thumb on her mug. "There were days that only thinking of you, what you would do in a particular situation, got me to the next day."

Stella knew her mouth had to be hanging open. "Me?"

AJ nodded and gave Stella a knowing grin. "You don't see yourself like everyone else sees you."

"I'm pretty sure I do." Stella squirmed under AJ's intense gaze.

AJ shook her head. "You're thinking of your brash exterior and colorful phrases. But you never let anything stop you. Every time I thought I was at my lowest, it was thinking of what you'd say to me. No pity parties."

"Well, not long ones anyway." Stella sat up. "You really see me that way?"

AJ squeezed Stella's arm. "You only have to look at how successful you are. You did all that yourself." She lifted her hand. "Of course, you had guidance over the years, but you're the one that made your business a success. No one else. And it's because you always get up and do what's needed."

Stella had no words and could only lift a shoulder in response.

"And what you did when I disappeared? Working with Adam. You have no idea what that meant to me. And it only proved how resourceful you can be."

"Don't get me started on your brother."

They both laughed as Stella wiped her eyes.

"I think we both learned something about Adam after that." AJ pulled her chair closer to Stella and looked out to sea.

After several moments of content silence, Stella glanced around. "Where's Maire?"

"Patrice was going to show her Sebastian's old office on the first floor and give her a more personal tour of the monastery than the rest of us got."

"With Maire busy and the men gone, that just leaves the two of us."

AJ leaned over the table and glanced around. "What did you have in mind?"

"Didn't you say you needed to find another way to the iron door?"

***

After another round of cider, AJ and Stella made a plan. AJ smirked. Not really a plan, more a last-minute crazy-ass thought after working up enough alcoholic poor decision making and false bravado.

Now, they walked, holding each other around the waist, to the rock wall. They stood like that for several minutes.

"You ready?" AJ asked.

Stella rolled her shoulders and bounced a couple of times like some prize fighter. "Yep, let's get this done."

They walked along the low wall, keeping their eyes on the bay, until it began to turn back toward the monastery. After a quick scan of the courtyard, AJ waited for Stella to climb over the wall. AJ followed then directed Stella to the left where another rock wall ran horizontally along the back of the monastery. The kitchen garden lay on the other side.

The cliff was as she remembered it. A gentle slope curved for thirty yards before it turned into a steep drop-off. From there, rock climbing skills would be required. This was the cliff she'd climbed that fatal night when she'd crawled over the rock wall and killed Dugan with a well-placed arrow.

"Follow the wall as far as it goes. They might have extended it over the decades."

The vegetation didn't appear much different than it had the last time she'd seen it this close. Although it had been dark at the time, and she'd been climbing up from the cliff. Vines and flowers grew along the wall where it bordered the courtyard, but as they ventured farther away, the local scrub brush took over.

They passed the kitchen, and the slope turned steeper as they walked. It didn't take long before her hopes were dashed. The terrain turned to rocky cliff in another twenty feet.

"Hold up. Step back here and stay as high as you can. I'm going to take a couple of steps down. If I stumble, don't move. I have the skills to stop myself, you don't." AJ glared at Stella.

"Fine. You don't have to give me the stink eye. I walked farther than I should have in the first place."

AJ breathed a sigh. "All right. I just wanted to be sure." Her friend's paler than normal face gave AJ all the assurance she needed that Stella wouldn't follow.

She felt the loose gravel under her shoes, and she reached for a bush, thankful there weren't thorns, and held onto it as she moved a little farther across and down. She didn't want to go any farther, but she had to get a good look at the cliff.

The ledge she'd walked that dark night was probably thirty to fifty feet down. It slanted across the face of the cliff, moving farther down the closer one got to the outer staircase that led to the bay. With the right equipment, she could get across the face. It appeared from this distance that the staircase still existed, but without binoculars she wouldn't be able to tell its condition. Even then, she wouldn't know if the stairs were viable all the way up to the landing and the iron door.

She turned back, slipping once and smiling at Stella's muffled cry. "I'm all right."

Then she was next to Stella, letting her walk in front. "It's as bad as I remembered, but I had to be sure."

"So that leaves the path from the road." Stella waited for AJ to walk next to her as the slope decreased. "Or from the inside."

Without any warning, Stella stumbled then straightened.

"What the..." AJ didn't finish the sentence when she glanced up and saw a man approaching them. She couldn't be sure, but his face looked red, and it wasn't nearly cold enough to blush cheeks, even with the light breeze off the bay.

"You can't be over here." The man's shout was loud enough to hear over the breeze, and his bluster continued as he drew nearer. "There's no path for you to walk. And you must have climbed over the wall."

When he reached them, AJ read his badge. Linus. He was the Cider House manager. She groaned. At least it wasn't one of the monks. This would be awkward to explain if someone in the monastery heard about their stunt.

"There aren't any signs that say not to walk over here." Stella smiled and then hiccupped.

It sounded real, and AJ gave Stella a quick glance. It was hard to tell what was real versus made-up. That had to be a good sign. Maybe this would work after all.

"We shouldn't have to have signs. It should be obvious it's dangerous."

"In America, there would be signs all over the place telling a tourist where not to go."

"I'm sure."

Stella tilted her head as if considering his response. Like it wasn't an obvious insult. Then she pointed at AJ, who wasn't prepared for the change in script. "She's a rock climber. This..." Stella flung her arms out to reflect the cliff behind them, and both Linus and AJ took a step forward, preparing for Stella's eventual tumble, but she auto-corrected and came back to an upright position.

Stella stared at them. "What's wrong?"

"I'm so sorry." AJ stepped forward to grab Stella's arm, finding it difficult to tug her back toward the courtyard. "We were gazing at the bay. I got lost in thought, and she got away from me." She waited next to him while Stella made several attempts to get over the wall.

"I'm afraid she had too many ciders." AJ gave the man an apologetic smile. "She's recently been through a divorce. Very messy." She shrugged. "Well, the holidays and all. When the family decided to follow our ancestor's journey to the monastery, we thought France would be good for her."

AJ wiped an eye.

"Oh, forgive me. I had no idea." The man appeared flustered. "That is horrible. I know your group will be visiting for another few days. I promise we won't mention another word about this."

"I really appreciate that." After giving him a tentative smile, she turned to find Stella stumbling toward the Cider House. She scrambled over the wall and called out, "I think we've had enough cider for today."

"Just one more," Stella yelled back.

AJ grabbed her before they made it back to the patio and turned her toward the parking lot. "I'm really worn out. Let's go back to the villa so I can take a nap. Then we can have more cider."

"All right." This time Stella was easy to drag back to the car. AJ glanced over her shoulder and found Linus watching them, hands pressed to his chest. AJ waved and received one in return.

"I think your performance might have been a bit over the top." AJ whispered before pushing Stella into the passenger seat.

When AJ got in, Stella grinned. "And yet, you had him apologizing for my outrageous American behavior."

She couldn't stop her own laugh. "You're going to give me a bad name."

"Oh, honey. I blame Finn for that."

7

Adam dropped another platter of his famous pancakes on the table, batting away Patrick's hand. "Don't use your hands. You're with company."

AJ stared at all the food. Adam, Helen, and Emory had been cooking all morning. She smiled at her mother, who was currently squeezing orange juice as Emory cut the oranges. Their heads were down, each whispering about who knew what. She didn't know what would come of their fling. Emory lived a couple hours away from Baywood. What would it be like to only have to worry about her mother's romance? She glanced at Maire, who stared out the window. This was the person she needed to worry about. Maire would get to see Sebastian's journal, but AJ knew it wouldn't be enough. Her friend was haunted by the past, by regrets.

Finn squeezed her shoulder and passed her a plate of sausage and bacon. "Don't fret over Maire. Ethan is doing enough of that for all of us."

AJ turned to Ethan. He was shoveling in pancakes as fast as Adam made them. "Are you trying to convince me that he's stress eating?"

"Oh, aye. You missed the part where he made a plate for her, and after she picked at the fruit and a piece of bacon, he finished her plate than put it back in front of her to make everyone think she ate it." He gave AJ his intoxicating grin as he deepened his brogue. "It's true love, it is."

She laughed and pushed one of his errant locks away from his eyes. "I always said you were a romantic."

Stella stumbled her way to the table. Her hair disheveled, her eyes half closed, she managed to sidestep Charlotte's dolls strewn across the floor. She fell into a chair and held up a hand. "No speaking to me until I've drunk a full cup of coffee."

Finn poured her a cup then made a plate for himself. "So, who all is going to see the journal?"

Madelyn worked her way around the table pouring orange juice. "Patrick, take your brother and sister and wash your faces and hands. Then get ready." The children jumped up from the table and raced for the hall as she continued to yell. "And pick up your toys and make sure you have your backpacks." She sat down and placed two pancakes on her plate. "I'd love to go, but I think this is a special day for Maire. She doesn't need it to be a zoo, which is exactly what would happen with the kids. Besides, Helen will be coming with me and the kids for a day at the marina. Adam found a ship that gives tours. But I'd love to see pictures tonight."

AJ shrugged. "I would think they'd let us take pictures, but who knows. Gallagher has that place locked down."

"I know Gallagher can be a stickler at times." Emory brought over a bowl of scrambled eggs and a fresh bowl of fruit. "When I first contacted him about the stones, he was very open about what they'd discovered. He was full of excitement. But when ownership of the artifacts came up and everyone stuck their noses in, it appears the stress got to him. He's a researcher not an administrator, but he also sees things as black and white."

"It is black and white." Maire sat up and turned toward the table. She might have appeared to have been in her own world, but as always, she knew everything going on around her. And there was a fire in her gaze as she glared at Emory. "The artifacts he's uncovering aren't in some unoccupied tomb or empty field. They're precious items from a working monastery—a piece of their past. Items that belonged to other monks. To think someone could just waltz in and make claim on them is no different than the monarchies of that time."

The room quieted at her outburst, and all eyes turned toward Emory. But he was nodding, a smile softening his expression as he pulled apart a croissant and buttered it. "Oh, my dear, don't get me wrong. I wholeheartedly agree with you."

Maire thinned her lips as her eyes narrowed. "You do?"

"Oh, yes. It's quite obvious to me, and based on what I've seen in other European countries, the courts will most assuredly rule in the monk's favor. But I also see it from a historian's point of view, which is the same as an archaeologist's." He took a bite of the croissant then added a dab of homemade jam that Helen had bought from one of the apple farms they'd visited. "When we find something of historical note, our first job is to authenticate and date it. Well, there's much more to it, but those are the highlights. And once all that is accomplished, we want to share it with the world.

"Now, there's two reasons for that, and one is entirely selfish. Our standing is only as good as what we've recently published. We want to show the academic world what we've found and get a pat on the back." His gaze held a twinkle. "We're not exactly in it for the money." Even Maire had to smile at that. "But we also have an intrinsic desire to share what we've discovered with the world at large. Everyone should have the opportunity to see history to better understand history. The best way to achieve that is through museums and the like."

Maire lowered her gaze and gave a half-shrug. "I can see your point."

"Maybe the monks should create their own museum. Then others can see what Gallagher and his team found. It could be another source of income for the monastery." Stella pulled over a clean plate and buttered the two hot-off-the-grill pancakes Adam dropped on her plate. Madelyn passed her the syrup. AJ had to smile. Somehow, Adam and Madelyn had adopted Stella into their family.

"That's an excellent idea." Emory finished his croissant, sipped coffee, then leaned back, elbows on the arm of the chair, he tented his fingers. "That might ease the tension between the two groups. It's not perfect, but it's a step."

"Patrice was thinking something similar, though it wasn't as broad. She was thinking they could keep the artifacts in a single room so the archaeologists could study them as much as they wanted." Maire took a pancake from the fresh stack, her enthusiasm growing. "That would be a worthy endeavor, as long as the monks kept control."

"They would require someone with the training to handle fragile artifacts," Emory said.

"They have that young monk who's been trailing after Gallagher and his interns." Finn glanced at Ethan. "What was his name? Brother Martin?"

Ethan nodded. "He was taking notes on everything. He even had a video recorder."

Maire and AJ turned to each other. This was someone they hadn't met yet but might be an excellent resource.

"Will he be there today?" Stella asked before sliding a glance to Maire and AJ.

AJ held back a snort. The three of them were becoming a solid team, each learning how to play off a situation. Who should lead and when to step back.

"Oh, I would think so." Emory pushed his plate away and moved his cup of tea in front of him. He poured more hot water then added milk. "While you're looking at the journal, Gallagher will be reviewing the next section of the ledger. He agreed to let me monitor. I'm not sure which event will hold the most interest for the young and eager monk."

"You mean he might want to spend hours staring at a cargo manifest rather than see if Maire can decipher Sebastian's journal better than the trained archaeologists?" AJ couldn't help it. She meant to stay unbiased, but the amount of energy being expelled over what was basically a large shopping list was staggering. She understood the importance of the ledger, but page after page of the same items, what else did they hope to find?

Emory gave AJ another smile which was becoming an affectation. Very rarely did the man ever frown. "Point taken. I always enjoy seeing how interns split themselves between events. To be honest, the room where the journal is stored is of average size, so only so many people can be in there before it becomes difficult to move about. And since the interns have already spent many hours on the journal, I'm sure they're ready to spend time with the ledger. Although, Gallagher will post a couple of interns in the journal room, as they are beginning to call it, just to keep an eye on it."

"You mean on us." Maire took a bite of pancake, her eyes brightening as she chewed, and she cut off a bigger portion.

"We'll just have to make sure they stay back." Ethan refilled his cup of coffee and those within his reach. "They have no business listening to our private conversations. Finn and I will make sure of that. Adam, I believe you're coming with us. We should be able to get you to the marina before the tour starts."

Adam nodded as he cleaned the stove, moving the griddle to the sink.

"So, six of us in all." Maire licked her fork. "These pancakes are truly amazing. And is this freshly made syrup?"

"From a farm just outside town." Helen began clearing dishes.

Finn stood. "Ethan and I will restock the SUV while you ladies finish your breakfast and get ready. Thirty minutes. We don't want to give Gallagher any excuse to change his mind."

———

M aire's stomach was in knots and the two pancakes she ate, which were delicious going down, now lay in a lump, unwilling to digest properly.

"Here." AJ passed her a bottle of water. "Drink up. It will settle your stomach. Don't argue."

Maire took the bottle. She had no energy to be disagreeable. After taking a few sips, she tightened the lid and stared at the monastery through the front windshield. Finn had parked facing the building, allowing everyone a moment to take it all in. There would be a confrontation today. Even with Brother Lucius forcing Gallagher's hand, nothing about the journal was ever easy. And while this conflict was nothing compared to what they'd braved before—an armed battle against deadly foes— there was a sense of urgency to discover what Sebastian had left for her. She couldn't provide any evidence. Only a gut-wrenching certainty there was critical information they needed to know, and she was the only one who could find it. She sipped more water and rolled her shoulders as she'd seen Ethan do a hundred times. A handful of archaeologists wouldn't stand in her way.

She ran her hands down her dress and took a large breath. Ethan took her hand, and she squeezed back. This was her larger worry. Once she found what she was looking for, what would she find within the pages? Her life was on a cusp. How long would Ethan follow wherever she led? She didn't want to be alone anymore, but she wouldn't be able to settle until the business with the stones were done. And no matter how much she ignored them, tried to normalize, a nagging dread always returned. She couldn't hide anymore. It was time to make decisions. She squared her shoulders and got out of the SUV. Without waiting for anyone else, she strode to the entrance. She'd entered the outer courtyard by the time she heard the last door close. Footsteps hurried behind her, and she leaned into Ethan when he wrapped an arm around her shoulder.

"I'm ready for this." She slipped an arm around him and smiled up at him. "I'm prepared for whatever is waiting for us."

"You are the strongest woman I know." He steered them toward the side entrance, nodding at the monk who opened the door for them.

They only waited a few minutes at the basement door before the rest of the group arrived with Gallagher, Brother Lucius, and Professor Emory.

Maire straightened and gave everyone a bright smile. "Shall we go?"

As if waiting for a signal, Patrice appeared and unlocked the door, stepping aside to allow Gallagher to lead them. The first level of the basement had been completely remodeled. No more stone walls or ceiling. The floors were tiled, the walls covered in drywall and paint, the light almost too bright. Maire paused halfway down the hall and waited for AJ.

AJ shook with light tremors. "The cell where the duke held Finn is now some kind of workroom, all bright and shiny." She took a deep breath and probably one of her counts to ten.

"Are you all right?" Maire asked.

After a moment, she nodded. "I'm okay. Let's see what else has changed."

Gallagher had turned left at an intersection. Maire glanced at AJ, who only shrugged. Halfway down this hall, they walked through another door and entered the tunnel that hadn't changed since Maire last walked the corridors. When they entered the third door to the right, Maire almost laughed.

Either the monks or the archaeologists had preserved this room, probably assuming this was Sebastian's secret room. In a way it was. He had several. There had once been a wall where they'd walked through the door from the remodeled area. The hidden door in the wall opened with one of the simplest locks— an old iron wall sconce. Just like in the black-and-white movies Ethan enjoyed.

She turned around and took in the room. This had been the largest of Sebastian's personal stores. He kept many files and a desk here, along with most of his herbs. Anyone could have confused this as an important room, and there was no doubt it held valuable artifacts. But not Sebastian's most precious items. Aged wooden bookshelves lined two walls, but a couple of metal ones had been added. She walked to the counter on her right and ran her hand along its length where she'd mixed dozens of tonics and tea blends with him. He'd always had stories to tell.

"Maire?" Ethan took her elbow. "The journal is over here." When she didn't move, he stepped closer and lowered his head. "What is it?"

"This isn't the room I thought it would be." Her whispered words couldn't hide her excitement. If this was the only room they'd found, Sebastian's most precious secrets were still safe.

"We know. We all realized it when we made that left, but you spent a great deal of time here." He waited, and she sensed his calm patience. "I don't mean to push. Take your time."

This was the moment. How strange that she'd walked directly to the counter rather than scan the room for the journal. She squared her shoulders and turned.

Everyone had filtered in and circled a table in the center of the room. If she leaned to her right and peered over Stella's shoulder, she could see the edges of a clear plastic box. Her heart thumped faster as she pushed past Adam and Patrice. The journal was laid open. She would be able to see his handwriting, read his words, and see what message he left her.

8

AJ stepped back, pushing Gallagher's intern aside to let Maire step in front of the case. Gallagher had left the man behind when he took Emory to see the ledger, and he'd been hovering over the case ever since. She still had to laugh at everyone believing this room was Sebastian's secret library. She'd only been in this room once when Sebastian had asked her help to move some books.

From what he'd told her, this was his backup workroom when the duke's men were searching the tunnels. The monk had four secret rooms filled with books and artifacts he considered it his job to protect. But his primary room—his library— was where he'd taken Maire and her the first time they'd met. And it was where they'd met each time after that. If Gallagher hadn't found Sebastian's library, then Maire would be itching to get in there.

"No touching." The intern's sharp tone snapped AJ out of her reverie.

"It's just a plastic case. She's not harming anything." Ethan's equally harsh response resulted in the intern taking a step back, though his lips pressed into a fine line and his eyes narrowed.

Ethan turned his back on him, laying a hand on Maire's shoulder as he leaned in. "Touch whatever you'd like and take your time."

Maire's only response was a slight nod. Her gaze never left the journal, and her lips moved as her hand ran from left to right as it slid down the case. When her fingers tapped the bottom of the case, she moved back to the top. This time, she moved slowly, occasionally pausing before continuing.

It appeared Maire had given the two pages a quick speed read before returning to move line by line as she interpreted his words. The shuffling of feet and pressing of other bodies made AJ step aside so Finn, Adam, and Stella could get a closer look.

The intern checked his watch, then tapped a foot. Gallagher hadn't mentioned a time limit, but the intern seemed to think otherwise. Brother Lucius must have had the same thought because he took the man by the elbow and moved him toward the door.

"If you have some other place you need to be, I'll be happy to monitor the group. Nothing else will be touched if that's what you're worried about."

"Professor Gallagher said you'd only be five or ten minutes." The man squared his shoulders as if preparing for a fight.

Brother Lucius's posture never changed, but he shook his head. "I'm not sure why he told you that, but we'll be here for a while. Once our visitors have each had time to review the journal, I'll want to read the pages myself. From what I saw at my first quick peek, Brother Sebastian wrote in French and Celtic. Breton Celtic I believe. It will take me some time to cypher it."

"I don't think that was what the professor had in mind."

"No. Probably not." His bland expression never changed, but his tone hardened. "Although I don't know why he wouldn't think we'd want to study what little he's allowed us to see of a journal belonging to the Brotherhood of Monks."

The intern swallowed and stepped back. "I'll have to ask him."

"Please. Go right ahead. I'm not sure your presence here is even required. But if you wish to stay, I suggest you pull up a chair." He turned to Ethan, who had also stepped back to let the others view the journal over Maire's shoulder. "I was thinking we might need a tea service. I'll walk this man back out so he can speak with Gallagher and get new instructions. That will give me the opportunity to order the tea."

Ethan walked to the door with them. "I'll see if I can find us a some more chairs."

After the intern was bustled out, AJ stepped back to the group. "Do you think they found Sebastian's library?"

"I doubt it." Maire tapped the glass in the far-right corner. "This would have been the easiest room to find. Sebastian was always curious why the duke never found it. He didn't move the more valuable items in here until after the duke was killed. Reginald, for as little time he spent here, was never interested in the tunnels, so Sebastian felt safe leaving artifacts here. But never the stones and certainly not *The Book of Stones*."

"You keep tapping at this corner." Finn wrapped his arm around AJ. "They look like symbols."

"I didn't realize I was doing that, but yes. Sebastian and I worked out a type of shorthand. We both worried our notes would be discovered and..." She laughed and ran her hands over the glass. "I guess we weren't much different than the druids. We wrote in Celtic and French, sometimes English. And we left codes that either pointed to other parts of the same journal, different journals, or The *Book of Stones* itself. The MM at the beginning of this particular symbol was his reference that I should pay attention."

"Your initials." Finn leaned closer. "The rest appears to be Celtic. I can make out a word or two."

Maire smiled. "Yes. See the symbol on the left page?" She tapped the lower corner of the glass. "It doesn't start with my initials so he's not pointing out anything I would find of interest, but I can tell he's referencing another book. It appears to be a French literature book." She shook her head then pointed back at the symbol on the upper right. "This symbol however is telling me to look at his journal dated April of 1805."

"That was several months after we left." AJ stepped closer, but other than recognizing Sebastian's tight scrawl and Maire's initials, she couldn't read any of it.

"What did I miss?" Ethan pushed his way through the door carrying four folding chairs which he opened and set around the room.

Adam filled him in. "Sebastian obviously thought you'd return. Where would this other journal be?"

"Most likely in his library," Maire said.

"I thought this was his secret office." Stella glanced around, lifting books and notepads as she moved around the room, occasionally stopping to read something.

Maire laughed. "This was his secret storeroom, but not where he kept his most valuable possessions."

"He kept a lot of stuff in here. His herbs and mixing bowls." Stella peered into one then grimaced and stepped back.

"Yes. He sometimes had to work in here if the duke's men were searching too close to his library."

"How do we get to his library?" Stella asked. "Hey, here's a map. It looks like it might be the tunnels down here. They have little Xs here and there."

Ethan and Finn studied the map. AJ leaned on Finn as she scanned the sheet that she recognized to be this floor. Two of the marks were in red ink, the other three in black.

"I don't know what the different colors represent." Finn tapped the map where the Xs were arranged. "The room we're in is this red mark." He pointed to the one farthest from the hall leading to the stairs. "The other red mark should be a room just around the corner."

"My guess is that they haven't found a way past points along this line." Ethan ran a hand along the width of the map. Then tapped a blank spot farther away from them and toward the mountain side of the tunnels. "It's not on this level, but one floor down there's a room here where the smugglers met."

AJ nodded. "That was where I met Jamie and Lando when I arrived with Beckworth. It's not far from the iron door."

Maire ran her hand down the map as Ethan had, along the main hallway from the staircase. "I think they were able to get past the secret door leading down to the next level. They might have reached Sebastian's library without knowing it. There's a statue of an ancient soldier that marks the entrance. Sebastian always referred to him as Christopher." She laughed. "He had such a wonderful sense of humor."

"So you could get to it?" Adam asked. "I mean. If no one was watching you."

She nodded.

Someone cleared their throat. "I'd like to introduce you to my assistant, Brother Desmond."

Everyone jumped when they found Brother Lucius standing behind them.

AJ studied his face. How long had he been standing there? For an old guy on the mend, he was rather stealthy.

"Sorry to startle you. I didn't want to interrupt." He glanced around the room then settled into the closest folding chair. "Brother Desmond, Sister Patrice, and I are the only ones in the monastery with keys to these floors. That was a hard-fought agreement with the archaeologists. The door remains open during the day then locked at six p.m. unless by prior arrangement. The door is opened again at six a.m. I would suggest you search for the room during evening prayers. The kitchen staff are typically gone by eight p.m. Unfortunately, that hour is too late for me to be skulking around in the lower levels."

No one spoke. No one wanted to be the one who validated what he'd most likely overheard. It could be risky if they admitted they wanted to sneak into the tunnels, even though his plan was perfect. The question was, what would they find, and would anyone snitch and tell the archaeologists?

"Parden me, Brother Lucius, but you must know we didn't know you had returned." Finn had read her mind and was pretty bold about it. "Whatever is in Sebastian's library, well, there might be items we'd rather nobody finds."

Instead of becoming cross or defensive, Lucius's eyes glimmered. "Yes, we are on the same page, Mr. Murphy. Professor Gallagher has already collected more than enough artifacts to last them years of study, if his obsession with a two-hundred-year-old inventory list is any indication." Lucius couldn't quite hold back a smile when Stella snorted. "Anyway, I would like to establish our own internal library of rare artifacts cared for by the monks. We were originally prescribed as holders of sacred objects. Not the owners, but as caretakers."

"Yes, I remember..." Maire caught herself, "...reading about that in the journals from AJ's ancestors. They must have thought it memorable to have noted it."

Lucius gave her a long look before glancing around the room. His gaze held AJ's before moving on to the next person. After a moment, he nodded. "Sister Patrice tells me you're aware of the differing opinions on who has the rights to the artifacts. The strange thing is that we would have been happy to lend the artifacts to museums and research facilities so long as ownership remained with us. But I understand man's need to make his mark in the world. I'm much too old to worry about such things for myself." He removed a handkerchief from his pocket and wiped his brow. "I've been at the monastery for over fifty years. Gave every ounce of strength and knowledge I'd been born with to help it survive. Seen dozens of monks come and go. Sisters, too. Although their convent is several miles from here. What I'm trying to say is that I have a personal investment in this place. With its bones, if you will. I'm indebted to the original duties asked of the Brotherhood centuries earlier. If Brother Sebastian felt it important to keep certain artifacts away from the rest of the world, he must have had his reasons. Although, I do admit, those reasons might no longer exist."

"And who would make that decision?" Finn asked.

Lucius smiled. "That is the question, isn't it? If only those who lived within the monastery knew of their existence then it would be the prior and his council, of which I am one of six in that position. I imagine input from other knowledgeable resources would bear considerable weight in the final decision."

Finn glanced at AJ, then Maire and Ethan. When no one spoke, he turned back to the monk. "Can you give us some time to discuss it?"

Lucius stood. "Of course. It's lunch time, and I am famished. Several of us meet at the Cider House in the afternoons after a day in the garden. Perhaps you can find me there."

He left as quietly as he'd come in, Brother Desmond following behind.

Finn clapped his hands. "Okay, while we're here, let's give Maire more time with the journal. The rest of us can do some snooping. We're looking for anything that mentions the stones or the books. You never know what the archaeologists might have overlooked. Try to leave things as you found them."

Adam strolled to a bookcase by the door. "I'll search this case and monitor the door. I can accidentally block it if someone tries to enter."

AJ searched with Finn. "What are you expecting to find?"

"Nothing, but it doesn't hurt to make sure we don't overlook anything. I imagine Sebastian hid anything about the stones and books quite well. But if we find something, we'll either need to bury it or trust its fate in someone else's guiding hands."

"That's a big risk."

"Aye, so let's hope Sebastian hid everything good and proper."

9

Waverly Estate - England - 1804

Beckworth, also known as the Viscount of Waverly, strode through the manor, running his finger along a side table, satisfied to see it dust free. He stopped to stare at the chandelier in the foyer, pleased to see the candles had all been replaced for the long evening to come. The staff always did an excellent job, especially when guests were coming. It would be a difficult few days for them.

When the only occupants in the manor were him and the staff, everyone relaxed and did their jobs with smiles and pleasantries. He left the running of the place to his butler, Barrington, and housekeeper, Mrs. Walker. He couldn't be bothered with it, not with his current activities. These days, he barely found time to hunt with his neighbors or visit Eleanor.

He sighed when Mrs. Walker stormed through the sitting room, a cross expression on her face.

"The grocery man is at it again. He sent mutton instead of

lamb." She straightened her shoulders, her stern face never changing.

"Relax, Mrs. Walker, the guests haven't arrived yet." He turned and walked toward the stairs that would take them to the kitchen. She followed on his heels. "You'll have plenty of time to act the perfectly stiff house servant once they arrive. I know how taxing it will be for everyone, especially during the holidays. Make sure everyone knows they'll have extra time off to celebrate in their own way as soon as everyone leaves. We all have our roles to play."

Her shoulders relaxed. "Thank you, my lord."

Beckworth sighed. She would never call him Beckworth. The staff would only relax to a point. "Let's see what Cook can do with the mutton until the grocer makes good. Maybe we should save that for when everyone is gone. There should still be some wild boar left over from last week's hunt."

"Yes, sir. Cook did mention that."

"Excellent. Crisis averted."

After confirming with Cook they would survive a weekend full of guests, he went back to the main floor and followed the hallways to the conservatory, bracing for the chilly air before exiting through the French doors. The rain had stopped before sunrise, but the dampness remained. Everyone would arrive under gray skies, but no matter, it was always a risk having a party at this time of year. The first guests shouldn't arrive for another thirty minutes, so he found a bench under an elm tree that was still dry. He unbuttoned his tailcoat and stretched back, giving his sleeves a light tug before reaching in a pocket to retrieve a letter he'd received a fortnight ago.

Beckworth,

Sorry for the quick missive. No time for pleasantries and such. Much to do.

I just visited an old tailor friend of mine. He recently received silk fabric from the East. I think you'll find it makes quite comfortable waistcoats in the style I know would be of interest. He's holding several varieties for you, but if you want anything for the new season, you'll need to visit him by the twelfth of January.

Your Friend,

H

Beckworth folded the note and tucked it back in his pocket. It hadn't been six months since his return with the Heart Stone, now safely in Hensley's hands, and already another request. The man ran a network of spies for the Crown, all very secretive. Finn Murphy—could he call the man a friend now—had worked for Hensley for years. Somehow, Beckworth found himself in the thick of them, and it intrigued him. He'd played games his whole life, always pretending to be someone he wasn't. This time, he'd be working for England, and for the first time in a very long time, the idea gave him a sense of purpose.

He'd been happy to return to Waverly, the first place he truly felt at home. But now that the duke, his half-brother Reginald, and Dugan were dead, and once he caught up his affairs for the months he'd been gone, he would have very little to do. His barrister and agent were quite competent with the affairs of the estate. And as much as Beckworth would like to consider himself a man of leisure, the lifestyle didn't fit well.

He tugged at his sleeves. It couldn't hurt to visit this tailor. No address was given, which meant his initial contact would be at the gentleman's club he frequented while in London. With the war with France still going strong, the mission could be anything. Maybe he'd learn more in the next few days.

"Sir, sorry to disturb."

Beckworth glanced up, not surprised he hadn't heard Barrington approach.

"The first of the guests are arriving. It's Dame Ellingsworth with Lord and Lady Osborne."

"Very well." He stood. Thank the heavens for Elizabeth. She would make sure everything ran smoothly. A true godsend, that woman. He took a deep breath. Only a few days and they'd be gone. But until then, appearances were everything, especially if he intended to play spy for England.

"Oh, Teddy, have you met Lady Prescott?" Dame Elizabeth Ellingsworth waved at Beckworth, who had just spent the last twenty minutes listening to two old army colonels, both now retired, explain how England could squash France and put Napoleon in his place.

If he could only find a quiet five minutes with a glass of whiskey. When he spotted the raven-haired beauty standing next to Elizabeth, his weariness disappeared. He tugged at his sleeves and accepted a glass of champagne from a passing footman.

He prepared his most charming smile and gave a slight bow when he reached the women. "I'm afraid I haven't." He racked his brain but couldn't remember inviting her. Who had she arrived with?

"Lady Prescott, let me introduce you to our host, Lord Theodore Beckworth, the Viscount of Waverly."

"Everyone calls me Penelope." Her voice was deep and sultry, and Beckworth's loins stirred.

He took her hand and kissed it. "And everyone calls me Beckworth."

Her brow lifted. "Not Teddy?"

He grimaced.

"Oh, no. I'm the only one able to get away with that." Elizabeth laughed.

"I'm so sorry for invading your gathering. I was visiting with

Lady Singleton and the earl when your invitation came." Lady Prescott fluttered her lashes and sipped her champagne.

He smiled, fascinated by the deep blue of her eyes, which was probably why he didn't miss her quick glance around the room. It might have been the normal perusal everyone did at these social events, wondering if there was someone more important or more socially connected they should be speaking to. But something nagged at him. And his street sense, that tingle from working the backstreets of London in his youth, never went away. Something told him there was more to this woman, but he wasn't sure if he should be wary or try to take her to bed.

"It's no problem." Beckworth tugged at his sleeves before meeting her gaze. "There are plenty of rooms, and the earl sent a note that he'd be bringing a guest. Now the mystery is solved." He dropped his gaze to her decolletage before lifting his eyes to hers, somehow not surprised to see a challenge in those blue depths. Perhaps the next few days wouldn't be as boring as he thought.

Barrington caught his eye, giving Beckworth a slight nod. More guests. He pulled out a silver watch and noted the time.

"I beg your ladies' forgiveness. It seems more guests have arrived."

Lady Prescott laid a hand on his arm. "I do hope we'll have more time to talk. Perhaps you can show me the gardens I saw from my room? Even in winter, they're quite lovely."

"The gardens are my pride and joy. Let's say tomorrow after breakfast?"

"I look forward to it."

Beckworth didn't miss the knowing gaze Elizabeth gave him as he turned to meet up with Barrington. She was always match-making for him. This time, she'd selected well. But something still bothered him as he strode toward the foyer. He'd have to find time for cigars with the earl and see what he could share about this woman. Those blue eyes held more than curiosity. They held intelligence and something else he couldn't name. And it was that something else that left him twitchy.

When he reached the front door, he stopped next to Barrington. "I need five minutes in my study."

"Perhaps your new guests will reinvigorate you, sir. I'll have a bottle of whiskey brought to your study."

Beckworth poked his head out to find a heavyset man step down from the newly arrived coach then turn to assist a short, round woman. He smiled. His shoulders relaxed, the knot in his stomach dissipated, and a smile lit his face. He pulled at his sleeves as he moved swiftly down the steps.

"Hensley, my good man, I wasn't sure you were going to make it."

The large man turned, but before he could say anything, Mary, his wife, pushed him out of the way.

"Teddy, I'm so sorry we're late. My, but don't you look dashing. That color is perfect on you."

When Mary reached him, she didn't wait on propriety. She grabbed his offered hand and pulled him in for a hug. She smelled of bottled roses and mint that on anyone else might be cloying. To Beckworth, the scent reminded him of family, and his eyes watered before he blinked them dry.

"I worried something kept you from coming." He stepped back but held onto her hands, giving her equal study. "You look stunning as always."

She batted his arm. "You always have the right words." She glanced at the butler. "It's Barrington, isn't it?"

He gave her a slow nod.

"Why don't you show me where everyone is while the men catch up?"

Footmen were already pulling trunks from the back of the

carriage when Beckworth noticed someone else getting out of the coach.

"We would have been here sooner, but we received a message that the *Daphne Marie* had arrived in Bristol." Hensley turned toward the coach. "It seemed easier for us to travel together."

Beckworth smile broadened when Jamie, the captain of the *Daphne*, and Fitz, his first mate, gathered around them. They all shook hands. "Excellent. I wasn't sure if my message found you."

"It was luck, really." Jamie patted Fitz on the shoulder. "If Fitz hadn't gone back to retrieve a couple barrels of rum that had been left on a wagon, we would have missed the messenger."

Fitz pulled at his collar and then his waistcoat. He grumbled. "And I'm beginning to think those two barrels weren't worth the cost."

The others laughed, which only made Fitz growl.

Beckworth glanced around. "What about Lando?"

"He's caring for the ship. You know how he gets around aristocrats." Jamie had filled out in the three months since he'd seen him. Now the captain of the *Daphne*, Finn Murphy's old ship, the young lad had proved himself several times. And the two of them had shared many long nights with conversation and a bottle of Jameson on their return from France.

Beckworth swung his arm toward another set of stairs leading to the front of the manor. "Let's go through the east entrance. I have a bottle of whiskey waiting."

"That's the best news I've heard." Fitz all but ran up the steps to the doors.

"Sorry, about Fitz. He didn't want to come." Jamie fell into step with Hensley and Beckworth.

"Which is why I made sure the invite included him."

"I'll warn you now, he only has that one good jacket and waistcoat."

"I'm sure Mrs. Walker can find something appropriate that won't chafe as much."

They quieted as they entered the foyer and quickly moved down a short hall to Beckworth's private study. The room looked more like a library with the tall stacks that filled three of the walls. Beckworth stepped aside when the men entered, and he directed Hensley to take his chair behind the desk.

"This is your home," Hensley protested.

"Yet somehow I'd feel out of place sitting there right now." Beckworth dropped onto a small sofa and sprawled out while a footman poured the drinks. "Thank you, Spencer, we can take it from here."

"Very good, sir." Spencer shut the door quietly behind him.

"You fit your role well." Hensley sipped the whiskey and must have found it to his liking as he took a longer swallow.

"I've been playing it long enough." Beckworth held up his glass in a mock salute.

Jamie and Fitz grunted in response.

Hensley held his glass up and stared at it. He turned it this way and that, as if dazzled by the way the light hit the amber liquid. "This weekend will be the first time I'll see you in action. I don't want to add any pressure to having a household of guests, but there's something brewing, and I think you could play a large part in our investigations."

Beckworth eyed the old man. Hensley wasn't one to wait on formalities, but his curiosity was piqued. He'd been happy enough to remain at Waverly and play manor host and viscount when he was under the duke's collar. Ever since he'd gotten involved with AJ and Murphy, something in him had changed. He had his friends, those he'd kept hidden from the likes of Dugan. But he wanted more, and at the time, he thought that meant money and power. Well, the money was still important. After growing up on the streets of London, one didn't spit at money and finer living. But power? That just spelled trouble. And damn it, now he wanted to help his country, his community. What the hell happened to him? He snorted and took a swallow of whiskey and choked back the burn.

"When did you hear that Gemini resurfaced?" Jamie sat up, elbows on knees as he focused on Hensley.

Beckworth was sorry to have been woolgathering, and rather than ask Hensley to repeat what he'd said, he waited for him to answer Jamie's question.

"About a month ago, maybe a fortnight before then." Hensley leaned back in the chair, his gaze focused on the ceiling. "There's been much going on with the war, so this would be a good time while the Crown is distracted."

"Where was this at?" Beckworth hadn't heard anything, but it had been several weeks since he'd been to London.

"That wouldn't have been too long after we returned from the monastery with the Heart Stone." Jamie glanced at Beckworth.

Beckworth shook his head. "I haven't heard a thing. Not even while I was in London. But I admit, I wasn't looking for information. I was busy getting my affairs back in order from being gone so long."

"And you don't remember anything suspicious while you were there, or perhaps on your way home?" Hensley put a light tone on his question, but Beckworth wasn't fooled. Hensley was looking for any tidbit he could find, or perhaps confirming which side Beckworth was on.

"Nothing. Do you think they're after the Heart Stone?"

"It might not have anything to do with the stones," Hensley admitted. "We only have speculation, though we're still convinced Gemini was the one who leaked information about the druid's book to your half-brother. Dugan knew of the stones, and maybe the book, but it was Gemini who stirred everyone up."

"Is this Gemini working for someone else?" Jamie asked.

Hensley took a moment to answer. "We don't know. The only thing we can confirm is that they have a lot of money backing them. Possibly someone with a great deal of clout as well."

Beckworth nodded. "That's the only way this could be kept so quiet. Unless..." What would he do if he'd become aware of the stones but didn't have the duke's money or connections? He'd think it mad and nothing more than a fairy tale. But what if he had proof, or was as nutter as the duke? He would still need a crew, preferably a large one to get anything done. They'd require money, but not necessarily anyone in power, especially if they were looking for that power themselves. Maybe it wasn't about power at all, but another way to earn a big payday.

"Well, out with it, man," Fitz grumbled. "Though I have no issues with just sitting here drinking this fine whiskey." He elbowed Jamie. "It mush be Irish."

Beckworth glanced at the men. "Sorry, I was just thinking. This might not be another duke trying to find a way to sweeten a deal with the king."

"Maybe it's someone working for France," Jamie suggested.

"Possibly." Hensley didn't sound convinced. "We've sent notes to our informants in France, but it will take weeks before we hear anything."

Beckworth couldn't explain it, but this felt different than what they'd been up against before. It was unusual for someone to keep their identity hidden for so long. Not everyone on a payroll could be trusted. But with nothing to go on except poking around until something squealed...no. There had to be a better way.

He stood. "Until we have more to go on or happen to stumble across something, I say we table the conversation until after the weekend. I've decided to have you stay in the east wing, away from the other guests, who will be staying in the west wing."

"I get it. You want to keep the riffraff separated from your finer guests." Fitz didn't seem bothered by it.

"My own rooms are in the east wing. I thought you might prefer the solitude. My study is available whenever you'd like. The staff will serve breakfast in the smaller dining room, or you can mingle with the other guests. Your option. But I do expect to see you for dinners and hunts."

Jamie and Fitz both appeared relieved.

"Mary will be more than pleased to have rooms in what she will assuredly consider her own wing." Hensley pushed himself out of the chair. "I'm afraid you're spoiling her."

"And no one is more deserving." Beckworth clapped Hensley on the shoulder. "She made me part of her family."

10

Waverly Estate - England - 1804

Beckworth let his steed run. Part of the hunting party had split off, following the scent his pack of hunting dogs had picked up. But he'd sensed movement off to the left and decided to follow his own nose. The hounds, only five in all, were trained well enough to keep his guests occupied, but the dogs preferred to chase fox over a deer. He'd lost the desire to chase animals that didn't put food on the table long ago. That had been back in the early days of working for the duke, when Beckworth felt a kinship with the hunted fox. He shook himself like a cat coming in from the rain and shifted his face into the wind in a vain attempt to scrub the unwanted memories clean.

He was the Viscount of Waverly and there was no one to challenge him anymore. All his ghosts were dead and buried. After another mile, he slowed his horse. The hooves and snorting of horses behind him made him smile. Not everyone was eager to follow the pack. He stopped and turned his mount around. Three riders walked their horses up to him.

"Lady Prescott, you don't care for the hounds? This isn't quite the gardens I promised you."

She turned her horse next to his. She sat straight and proud, handling her horse as she did the suitors who followed her around Waverly like lap dogs. "I had the feeling you might have caught the scent of something larger."

He studied the woman. Barely a hair out of place, her cheeks were flushed from the sun and wind, and her luscious red lips were slightly parted as she breathed, her bosom rising with each breath. She was fetching. The intelligence in her gaze didn't bother him as it would many others. But that slight flicker he caught when he peered deeper screamed caution. And that was enough to draw his interest.

His smile widened, and he tugged at a sleeve. "I'd seen movement to the left when the hounds turned toward the river. But I'm afraid it was nothing. By then, it felt good to just let the horse run."

"Then perhaps we should rejoin the group."

Beckworth glanced at the man who spoke. He'd settled his mount several feet behind Lady Prescott. Beckworth couldn't remember his name, but he'd seen him around Lady Prescott several times since his arrival. He couldn't quite recall when the man had arrived, but it couldn't have been more than a few hours after her. Lady Prescott spent time flirting with most of the men, but this particular guest had been following her around more like a guard than a suitor. Or perhaps a partner?

"I think Beckworth was on to something. I say we push on to the left, down toward those elms." Fitz pulled at his cravat and scratched his chest. Beckworth hid his grin at the first mate's discomfort.

"It's nothing but a waste of time," the other man said.

Beckworth turned to study the area Fitz suggested. It was a perfect spot for deer. A small lazy creek formed a pond the wildlife enjoyed. His heart wasn't in it, but it would do Fitz good.

Lady Prescott gazed at Fitz and there was challenge in her blazing blue gaze. "Shall we see which of you is right?" With a wink at Beckworth, she added, "And we'll find time for those gardens." She turned her horse toward the copse and gave it a slight nudge with her heels that sent her flying down the grassy field.

Within seconds, Fitz was on her tail. The other man gave Beckworth an irritated glance before pursuing. He laughed, and it felt good. And he was positive it was his mirth-filled voice and the scent of the chase that flushed the deer out of hiding.

L ater that afternoon, Beckworth entered the solarium dressed in tan breeches and a paisley waistcoat that matched his burgundy tailcoat. He was invigorated from the hunt and didn't mind that Fitz was the one to bring down the deer. He'd be sure Jamie left with a sizable portion of it salted and packed for the ship.

He glanced around and noted that most of his guests were enjoying an afternoon of games. Clouds filtered the winter sun, but it was dry and a brave few walked the gardens. There were two tables of whist, one being led by Elizabeth, one of the few card players he'd ever lost to. Lady Agatha, who'd learned from Elizabeth and managed the second table, would play better if she stopped ogling the men in search of her next conquest. As long as they didn't play for money, the guests at those tables would be in good hands. On the other side of the room, Jamie played chess with Hensley and a second chess set had been added for Lord Stuart Osborne, Lady Agatha's elderly husband and Lord Edgar Melville.

Other guests relaxed in conversation and two women worked on their embroidery. He was tempted to sit with them to hear the latest gossip but decided against it when he noticed Barrington close. His stalwart butler enjoyed gossip more than Beckworth. Satisfied the guests were settled, he searched the room again for Lady Prescott. She was probably resting after a hard ride and successful hunt.

He poured himself a glass of whiskey and watched Elizabeth and her partner win two games before Lady Prescott strode into the room, a pleasant flush to her cheeks. She gave him a quick glance and a smile before turning toward a group of men and women who were putting on shawls, preparing for a stroll through the gardens. Before she waltzed out the door with them, she gave Beckworth a saucy wink. If he didn't know better, he'd say she'd just had a tumble. But the thought evaporated when Fitz bounced in just as Lady Prescott exited.

Unable to leave his guests, his gaze turned to Osborne and Melville, their heads bent over the chessboard. Melville was in parliament and was always good for rumors. And Beckworth might discover a bit more about Lady Prescott. He pulled up a chair and situated himself between the two men.

After Melville's second move, he glanced over at Beckworth. "I heard it was a successful hunt. We should have followed your nose rather than the hounds."

Osborne laughed. "I would have put money on that. Beckworth has a sixth sense when he's on a hunt."

"I'll have to remember that."

"How goes the war effort?" Beckworth asked.

He half-listened to the two men discuss different strategies while he watched the room. He added a comment when he deemed it necessary but didn't hear anything new with the exception that Lord Langford, one of the war ministers, had a meeting with the king. Langford was an old friend from a lifetime ago and soon to be the father-in-law of Elizabeth Ratcliff, who was destined to be the first Keeper of the Heart Stone. A meeting with the king would mean a definitive change in strategy. Beckworth had to visit London. He felt out of touch. He'd take Hensley's advice in the note to heart and leave for London right after the new year.

A moment later, the man who'd followed Lady Prescott on the hunt entered the room.

"Melville, tell me, who is that man who just entered? I seem to have forgotten his name." Beckworth didn't look at the man and Melville gave him a quick nod.

"Beckworth can't remember a name." Osborne's laugh turned into a dry cough that he covered up with a handkerchief. "I can't remember the last time that happened."

"Which is why it's driving me mad." Beckworth pulled at a sleeve.

"I can't say that I know, either." Melville moved a knight. "Check." He lifted his head and gave the man, who poured a glass of wine then joined a couple of men by the hearth, a more thorough study. "Ah, he arrived the same time as us. We met as we turned into the drive. I can't recall his name. Give me a minute."

Osborne focused on the board and how to get himself out of a checkmate. "He was only introduced to me after dinner last night. Something with a G."

"Hmm. Yes." Melville sat back, his face lifting toward the ceiling, eyes closed. "Gaines. Mr. Gaines. No title that I could remember. Said he was friends of the Singletons."

Beckworth turned to watch Gaines. "Aren't those the friends of Lady Prescott?"

Osborne looked up from the board, a knowing grin on his

face. "I wondered when her name would come up. She rather fancies you."

Beckworth chortled. "Everyone likes to please the host.

"That's true enough." Osborne moved a bishop.

It was a hopeless move as Melville slid his bishop in place. "Checkmate."

Osborne sat back. "Well, I suppose I should be happy with my first win. Another go?"

Melville chuckled. "If you have the stamina for it. But I think a refreshment first."

Beckworth waved for a footman to serve the drinks then watched Gaines move silently through the room before setting down his glass and ducking out to the gardens. Beckworth strode toward the door and grabbed the arm of a passing housemaid.

"Are you in a hurry, Libby?" Beckworth asked.

"No, my lord. Mrs. Walker asked me to check the linens."

"See that man over there." He nodded toward Gaines, who strolled down the center path of the gardens.

She nodded.

"Tell me if he meets up with Lady Prescott. And if he does, how long they talk. I'll have Mrs. Walker ask someone else to check the linens."

"Very good, sir."

He couldn't have been more pleased. Libby was one of his best spies. No one ever suspected the mousy-looking housemaid. More's the pity for them.

11

Waverly Estate - England - 1804

Two hours later, a knock at Beckworth's bedroom door surprised him, but he nodded at his valet, Nigel, who was about to help him into his tailcoat. When the valet went to see who was there, Beckworth ventured out for a brisk turn on the balcony. The sound of the musicians warming up lent a magical note to the gardens that had been lit with dozens of lanterns. Even from this distance, he could smell the aromas drifting up from the kitchen. So far, the weekend had gone well. Everyone seemed relaxed, enjoying themselves with good company, excellent food, and the best spirits in the valley. What else could these stuffy aristocrats need?

One more day and he could stand at the front door and wave as they all left him in peace. It was his own doing, but it was wise to keep up the charade he'd carefully established four years ago when he first assumed the role as viscount. Now that dealings with the duke and Dugan were behind him, and his half-brother dead, he could do anything he wanted without fear of reprisal.

He sighed. Within a fortnight, his duties as viscount would be squared away after his absence. If Hensley passed him the occasional small job like gathering information in discreet circles, he would have more than enough time to hunt, visit friends, and continue to host these small gatherings. As a member of the nobility, he'd be expected to travel to London several times a year, time which could also be used to dig around for whatever Hensley might need. He'd already been considering purchasing a house in London for the season. But that came with its own problems and more parties to host. If he were to ever find a wife—a slight shiver passed over him at the thought—then he could leave all that formality to her.

No. Until his time working for Hensley was done, and that could be a month or several years, depending on when he tired of the game, then he'd give consideration to finding a second house and a suitable wife. Until then, the gentleman's club in London would suit him well enough.

"Sir, Libby would like a word."

"Thank you, Nigel. Show her in and give us five minutes."

When Libby entered, she kept her head down until Nigel closed the door behind him. Her head snapped up, and she gave Beckworth a nod.

"I wouldn't mind a quick nip before going back to my duties, sir."

Beckworth was already pouring two fingers of whiskey for the maid. He handed it to her and waved to the small sofa. She plopped down and dragged her feet up to the footrest. She sipped the whiskey and blew out a deep sigh.

"Who are you serving this weekend?" He sat in the chair next to the sofa and faced the warm hearth.

"Lady Agatha."

"That explains the sore feet. Had I known better, I'd have asked Mrs. Walker to assign you to Lady Prescott."

"Lady Agatha asked for me. I'm not sure she would have taken no for an answer."

"At least she's predictable."

"I'd say." She fanned herself and took a long sip.

"So, she found time for a dalliance?"

Libby chortled. "She rang for me at two am. Saw her coming from the east wing."

"Our young captain?"

Libby shook her head and giggled. "The first mate."

"Fitz?" He threw back his head and laughed. "Why doesn't that surprise me?"

"The more rigid and lofty, the farther they fall when it's time for games between the sheets."

"Truer words." He poured another finger of whiskey into Libby's glass. "So, what of our Mr. Gaines?"

"You were right. It took a while. Those two are being very careful. He wandered through the whole garden until stopping at the grotto. It was another five minutes before Lady Prescott showed."

"They didn't see you?"

She shook her head. "Those hedges are too thick, even in winter, unless you know where to stand. It was enough to peak through, but they were too far away to hear anything. They sat side by side with enough distance between them. All quite proper. They couldn't have talked more than a minute or two before Lady Prescott left."

"Did they look like lovers?"

Libby considered the question while sipping her drink. "If I had to put a name to it, it appeared more of a check-in. They definitely knew each other, but it didn't appear to be any romantic dalliance. They didn't touch once. That doesn't mean anything, but it is the most isolated spot in the garden."

Beckworth wasn't surprised, though he was disappointed. Why were all the gorgeous and available women up to something? It was likely Lady Prescott was searching for a wealthy husband, and while he wasn't as affluent as many others, he was younger and better looking than most. He was considered a catch from what Elizabeth and Eleanor told him, if they could be believed.

"I can keep my eye on him, sir. No one would give it any mind for a lowly housemaid to have dreamy eyes for a young handsome man."

He stared at the fire before turning to Libby. "Be discreet. But if they meet again, let me know."

He stood. "Finish your drink then be on your way. I have no doubt Agatha is probably screaming to know where you scampered off to."

"No worries, sir. I have her dress being pressed now." She stood and drained her drink. She reached into her pocket and took out a piece of candy that she popped in her mouth. "But if I don't start on her hair soon, she'll be spitting mad."

Libby scurried out, and Nigel entered with Beckworth's tailcoat.

"Let's finish this. I have a feeling it's going to be a long night."

———

Beckworth watched the inner and outer doors to the solarium and listened with feigned interest to Elizabeth, who regaled Mary and Lady Melville about her spring garden party. He'd listened to Elizabeth share the event so many times his nods and automatic responses were enough to leave the impression of attentiveness. They stood near a wall far enough away from the musicians to carry on a reasonable

95

conversation, and where he could monitor his guests coming and going.

He hadn't seen Gaines all evening, and he'd only caught a few sightings of Lady Prescott. Libby wandered through once, but she never made eye contact with him. Unable to do anything else with that situation, he turned his attention to his other guests. He'd made it a point to have little contact with Hensley or Jamie other than what a host would normally do, and he'd been surprised when Barrington mentioned that Hensley had received a messenger earlier in the day. He planned on waiting until after his other guests left before speaking with Hensley, but he was so bored he didn't see any harm in at least chatting with the men. While it wasn't good to hover around them all weekend, ignoring them would be unseemly of a good host.

A footman at a nearby serving table signaled him, offering him the perfect opportunity. "Ladies, I hate to interrupt, but it appears a footman needs my attention. Please enjoy the music."

Mary blushed and waved her fan while Lady Melville nodded. He bowed his head and was only a couple steps away when Mary's voice reached him.

"The viscount is such a perfect host. Even with a manor filled with guests he personally works with the staff to make our weekend more enjoyable."

"Yes, I'd heard good things about him before his long absence. He does seem to make one feel at home." Lady Melville's response would have made him preen if he didn't have so many other things to think about, but he managed a smile.

He handed his empty glass to the footman and asked for a refill. "Make it a double."

"Very good, sir." The footman glanced around and, as he poured, whispered, "Libby has a message for you."

"Go on." Beckworth kept his eyes on the room as the footman poured the whiskey.

"Gaines was seen heading into the garden. Libby has been detained by Lady Agatha, who requires a change of shoes."

Beckworth pulled at his sleeves and mumbled under his breath, "Bloody hell, can't the woman change her own shoes?"

The footman forced back a grin and offered the serving tray with Beckworth's refilled glass.

Beckworth couldn't help but chuckle at the footman's struggle. "That will be all, Donald."

"Very good, sir." The footman turned with a new tray of champagne and headed into the crowd.

Beckworth noted that Lord Melville had joined Elizabeth. Hensley and Jamie were still alone by the hearth, apparently watching two couples dance. Beckworth stopped for a polite moment with two other groups before stepping next to Hensley, who by then was in the middle of a hearty laugh.

"Oh, Beckworth. We were just talking about that time Fitz lured Lando to that brothel that was owned by an old friend of Lando's."

Jamie shook his head. "He wasn't a friend. Lando swore he'd kill the man if he ever saw him again. I arrived late, and all I saw were dozens of half-naked beauties running from the building." He laughed until tears shined. "I thought we'd have to break them both out of Newberg."

Beckworth laughed with them. While he'd never heard the story, he knew those involved enough to understand the humor of it. After a moment, and a quick scan around the room, Beckworth chanced to quell his curiosity. "I hear you had a messenger today."

Hensley continued to smile, but his tone turned serious. "Yes. I received news that Gemini is on the move again."

Beckworth's smile faded. It was bad enough to hear Gemini was still around and no one had figured out his identity. Now he was on the move again? And this was the wrong place to ask how they knew when Gemini was active if they didn't know who he was.

There was no doubt in his mind that Dugan had told Reginald everything he knew about those blasted stones, but he hadn't been aware anyone knew of the druid's book, also known as *The Mórdha Stone Grimoire*. From what Hensley's spies had uncovered, they believed someone called Gemini, who had eluded everyone for years, might have been involved. He hadn't given it another thought once Reginald and Dugan were gone and he had his estate back.

"Would it be possible for you to extend your stay an extra day? Most of the guests will be leaving tomorrow afternoon." As much as he wanted to put the stones and books behind him, Beckworth wanted a full report on this Gemini fellow if there was any chance of further trouble.

Hensley lifted a brow at the offer and glanced at Jamie.

Jamie shrugged. "I have a cargo run to Dublin, but it can wait another day."

Hensley scratched his belly as he glanced to where his wife was still standing with Elizabeth. "That would allow Mary to accept Dame Ellingsworth's invitation to spend time at her home to discuss a garden party. I'm afraid it was dangerous introducing those two."

Beckworth smiled. "Those two will be good for each other, but there might be more parties in your future."

Hensley frowned, then shook his head. "If it keeps Mary occupied, it's a small price. Now, tell us, Beckworth, where will tomorrow's Christmas Day hunt take us."

Beckworth, savvy enough to pick up the change in Hensley's tone, turned to see what created the man's abrupt change in subject. Lady Melville strode toward them with Lady Prescott and a determined expression.

The men bowed their heads.

"Sorry to interrupt what I'm sure is exhilarating conversation." Lady Melville stopped to catch her breath then gave them a bright smile. "We have the pleasure of such fine music this evening but there seems to be a shortage of men." She looked around as if to make a point.

Without wasting a moment, Jamie gave a more thorough bow, then held out his arm to Lady Melville. "And it would truly be a shame to leave a beautiful woman alone with such grand music."

Lady Melville blushed, and Beckworth did everything he could to not roll his eyes—a horrible behavior he'd spent the last few months trying to stop. Blast AJ and her influences, yet he smiled at her memory, mildly wondering what her and Murphy were up to. Then he shook his head. They wouldn't be up to anything for a couple more centuries.

He noticed Lady Prescott staring at him. He pulled away from her mesmerizing gaze, not sure he wanted to spend any time with her. She was up to something, and until he had time to do his own investigation, he'd come to the decision to not pursue a dalliance. Curious regarding her motives, it would be more interesting to play hard to get and see if she continued her pursuit. But that wouldn't get him out of his current social problem. Then a miracle walked toward him, and it was all he could do not to laugh.

"Ah, Mr. Fitzpatrick. The ladies were looking for dance partners, and Lady Prescott is in need."

Fitz pulled at his cravat then gave her a leering smile. "My pleasure, as always, m'lady." He gave a crooked bow and held out his arm.

"Sorry, my dear," Beckworth said. "A good host never strays from his guests."

Lady Prescott forced a smile and took Fitz's proffered arm. "Until next time."

When they moved away, Hensley leaned close. "That was a close one. Is there a reason you're avoiding her?"

"I haven't decided yet." But the lady's last look as she turned away said enough. They were far from completing whatever she was planning.

12

A J pushed back the remnants of her fish and chips, a few chips all that remained, and rubbed her stomach. Guerin's didn't have food like this the last time she'd eaten here. But Finn had been right. Not much had changed with the building itself. The room had been expanded to allow more tables, and a wall had been lengthened for the multiple beer and cider taps.

The large hearth remained and was keeping them pleasantly warm. Stairs still led upstairs, but the server mentioned the upper floors were private now. And while the place was simply another pub, it was still called Guerin's Inn. Regardless of the upgrades, she pictured Finn's crew sitting around the table, everyone laughing or grumbling, depending on whether they'd had a good day or bad. The memory that stuck the most was after the last battle with the duke, shortly after she'd stabbed Beckworth. Guerin had cooked a large meal for the men's return, which would have been more victorious except for their losses. It still hurt when she thought of Thorn and Dodger dealing with the death of Peele. Neither of them fully recovered from that loss.

She blinked away the tears and met Maire's shimmering gaze. So many memories.

"I say we let the women do their shopping while we go back and get a better look at that old ship they have." Ethan finished his mug of beer and leaned back, his hand grasping Maire's. "Unless you'd like to go with us."

Stella frowned. "I'd prefer to stay away from ships right now." She still looked a little green from their earlier boat trip down the coast.

The entire group had jumped in the three rentals after breakfast for a day of sightseeing and shopping. They'd agreed everyone needed time away from the monastery. There was nothing to do there until they met with Brother Desmond the following afternoon. Their first stop had been an apple orchard and then an old dairy famous for its cheese. When they arrived in town, Finn booked the group on a tour boat. The day was partly cloudy with a bit of wind, but the ship had a large indoor cabin for tourists to stay warm. It was a pleasant trip for everyone except Stella, who got seasick easily. AJ felt bad, especially when Stella could barely tolerate a bowl of soup for lunch.

After the group left Guerin's, Finn, Ethan, and Adam took off toward the marina, while the women, children, and Emory huddled to make afternoon plans. Madelyn and Helen thought the children had a long enough day, so Emory agreed to drive them back to the villa, leaving AJ, Maire, and Stella on their own.

"I didn't think it was going to be that easy to get rid of the men." AJ glanced toward the marina.

"They did seem rather eager to see an old ship. Didn't they go to the marina the other day?" Stella dug around in her purse until she found a pack of gum. Something she'd claimed eased her stomach.

"Any other time, I'd say men can look at the same ship every day and never get bored, but it did seem a bit suspicious." Maire pulled her sweater tighter. "Let's get away from the docks. The wind is too bitter. Besides, we have our own secret shopping to do."

"We should probably do a little Christmas shopping." AJ hadn't bought anything for Finn yet. Their first true Christmas together, and she'd given little thought to it. Once again, she questioned the wisdom of returning to the monastery for a family vacation. It had seemed like a logical step. Everyone still spoke of their time travel, now that Madelyn and Helen knew of it. And though it wasn't spoken much in front of Emory, it was impossible to watch their words whenever he traveled over from Eugene to visit with Helen.

"We can shop while we search for the items on our list." Maire strode up the street, a woman on a mission as the other two trailed after her. "At least we didn't have to think of a ruse to get away from everyone."

"Good grief. You realize we're here on a family vacation, but we spend most of it apart." AJ glanced through the window of the first shop along a street that housed dozens of stores vying for visitors' attention. How different from the tiny port village she remembered so well.

"We're together for breakfast, dinner, and all evening. I had no idea Emory played a flute." Stella pulled the three of them into a dress shop.

"Or that he'd bring it with him." Maire held up a dress before scrunching her face and putting it back. "But he does play well, and quite surprising how many Irish ballads he knows."

"He is a specialist on Celtic lore." AJ stared out the window and studied the other shops while Stella roamed.

After one circle of the store, the group wandered up the street, their perusals turning toward Christmas.

"It's a shame the house doesn't feel like it's the holidays." Stella found a scarf at a knitting store. "Your mother loves sitting on your deck, but she always complains about the cool breeze on her neck. She can keep it at your place on one of the hooks you put by the French doors."

"Great idea." AJ led them through an antique store she'd been dying to visit since their first drive through town. "This would have been our first holiday to decorate the inn."

"Oh, honey," Stella rubbed AJ's back. "Next year will be better after Jackson finishes the first-floor remodeling."

AJ laughed. "He would have just grumbled having to work around the boughs of holly."

"Do you think Finn would like this for his office?" Maire picked up a ship's bell.

The three of them spent an hour going through the antiques with AJ providing what guidance she could. When they continued on, they decided to finish their holiday shopping before focusing on their other list until they saw the general store.

"That's exactly what we needed," Maire said.

"My feet are killing me. There's a bakery two doors down." Stella grabbed both women and turned them in that direction. "We can do the general store after we rest."

"They only have two boxes of white left." Adam shuffled the boxes around. The shelves were in disarray after a young couple had mulled over their own decision, walking away with a single box. "Oh, here's a third one."

Finn glanced at the shelves, completely out of his element.

"Grab those, and these multi-colored ones will work." Ethan grabbed other items off the shelf and tossed them in the shopping cart.

"I was thinking a couple of spotlights. I think they were just around the corner." Finn strode in that direction but stopped when he noticed the mini tool kits. He squatted down and read the labels—a screw-driver, a hammer, wrenches, and other odds and ends. They would only need to buy nails. Unsure which one was better, he stood to show the two sets to Ethan and Adam. Ethan pointed to the one in his right hand while Adam pointed to the other. No help there.

Finn couldn't make up his mind and set them down, deciding to run over and grab nails while he considered the tool kits. He was gone for five minutes and found the men in the same spot, still glaring at the shelves. He would have expected Adam to be better at this. From what Jackson had told him before the group left for France, this was the men's specialty at this time of year. A tradition in the Jackson family.

"Did either of you think it strange the women didn't argue about splitting up for the rest of the afternoon." Ethan walked farther down the aisle, picking up a box, turning it to read the label on all sides, then setting it down before moving on to another item.

Finn checked his watch. They still had two more stops to make. "Aye. They're up to something."

"Really?" Adam dropped six boxes of lights and two spotlights in the cart. "I just assumed they wanted to shop on their own. You know. Christmas shopping for others is supposed to be a secret."

Ethan gave Finn a satisfied grin. "I already got something for Maire."

Finn returned the smile. "And I have something for AJ."

They both glanced at Adam, who appeared somewhat

sheepish. "I picked up something at the maritime museum for the boys and Madelyn found something on one of their drives for Charlotte."

"And Madelyn?" Finn asked. When Adam's face flushed, he grinned.

"I know what I want to get her, I just haven't found it." He shrugged. "I saw a shop down the street that might have it."

Ethan peered into the shopping cart. "I think we have everything we need. Finn and I can finish up. Go check the shop then meet us at the car."

"That would be great. I won't be long." Adam all but flew out of the store.

Ethan shook his head. "It took me weeks to think what to get Maire, but I found it just before we left for France. It was a bit of a chore getting it here."

Finn raised a brow but decided not to ask. "It was just the opposite for me. I've been planning and preparing her gift for weeks and thought about giving it to her before we left, but it will be worth the wait." Buying her the journal and quill when they'd been in Ireland had been so easy. It was obvious from the start she needed one. But he had no idea how much she would cherish it. Even though the pages were filled with her far-fetched time travel story and a list of items that would one day become antiques, the journal held a special place in their library. If someone were to read it years from now, they would think them both mad. He chuckled. "The more I get to know AJ, it's sometimes harder to find something that I think will please her. She's not interested in diamonds and expensive trips." He shook his head. "I think all they want is something to show them you care. That you've come to know them. So, even the most ordinary of trinkets, if it's important to her, is all you really need."

Ethan slapped him on the back. "Are you saying that simple observation is all that's required?"

"That and taking the time to shop." Finn couldn't help but give Ethan his best lopsided grin.

Ethan threw his head back and laughed. "And there's the rub. Shopping."

They were still chuckling as they left the general store with multiple bags.

"We shouldn't have let Adam run off until we got the bags to the car." Ethan stopped to shift the four bags he carried.

"Let's go back the way we came through the alley in case the women are around here."

"Good idea."

They turned left and kept a quick pace back to the car where Adam waited.

"Already found something?" Finn asked as he dropped the bags next to Ethan's while Adam raised the back door of the rental.

"Yeah. I knew they'd have something based on their window display." Adam picked up two bags and placed them in the SUV. "I'll give you some sage advice, gentlemen." He hefted two more bags in before turning to Ethan and Finn. "It's all about knowing your woman. It's not about the price, it's about what she likes. Take Madelyn for instance. She loves flowers. She'll buy bouquets to set around the house. So, you'd think she'd be happy if I brought her a bouquet. Not so. I learned that years ago. If I think I'm in the doghouse, I bring her a new kitchen gadget or new garden tool. I watch what she uses and, now here's the trick, I listen to her complaints in the kitchen when she can't get something to work right. Or see what tools are worn. Now she also wears jewelry and loves collecting things. So I find little charms and such that she can put on a necklace or bracelet. See. It's all about getting to know your woman." He beamed as he placed the last of the bags in the car.

Ethan glanced at Finn.

He couldn't help but shrug. "I told you. But the one thing I think we can all agree on, and have learned the hard way, no secrets."

Adam shuddered. "Never again."

"And what about what we're doing now?" Ethan asked.

"This isn't a secret, it's a surprise." Finn picked through the bags.

"Exactly." Adam stepped next to Finn. "What are you looking for?"

"I forgot the tool kit."

"We'll need that," Ethan said.

"Aye. It will be quicker if I go back and get it on my own. I'll be ten minutes at the most."

A J set down her coffee and a platter of mixed bakery treats. Stella had given AJ and Maire the job of getting anything they wanted so long as it came with coffee. She'd found a window seat, and AJ took a seat next to her. Maire followed with a mug of tea and Stella's coffee.

"How are your feet?" AJ cut each bakery item into three pieces, placed one of each on a napkin, then pushed it in front of Stella. "You look like a zombie."

Maire took her portion. "That's not true." She licked frosting off her finger. "I'd say more like one of those half-lifeless crabs that crawl out of the tidal pools on a sunny day."

"Well, it's good to know who your friends are." Stella rubbed her stomach. "I knew better than to get on that boat."

"You should have gotten ginger herbal tea instead of coffee, or peppermint if you don't like ginger." Maire had already finished off a sample of cheesecake and apple strudel. "I don't have anything with me, but I have something at the villa that will help."

"If I can wait that long."

AJ pushed the desserts closer to Stella. She'd only gotten seasick once, and that had been on the *Daphne* when they'd got caught in the storm off Ireland. So, she could commiserate.

Stella tasted the cheesecake, waited ten seconds, then finished it. She shrugged. "That seemed to go down fine."

"That wasn't long enough for a proper test." Maire laughed.

"Well, now it's been what, almost thirty seconds since I ate that. Long enough to try the next piece." Stella plopped a chunk of oatmeal cookie into her mouth, and halfway through chewing, gave them a thumbs-up.

AJ snorted. "Looks like she's getting her stamina back." She broke off a piece of strudel. "So what did you get Ethan for Christmas?" AJ hadn't bought anything for Finn yet, but she'd seen something at the antique shop she couldn't stop thinking about.

"I found two Celtic language books at the antique store." Maire played with a lock of hair, sharing a tentative smile.

"Was that for Ethan or for you?" Stella laughed. "I like those types of gifts. A two for one deal."

"It's not like that." Maire blushed with a lift of her shoulder. "Ethan is interested in learning Celtic."

"I didn't know that." Although it didn't surprise AJ that Ethan would want to share Maire's interests.

"Until now, he's only learned private words." Maire's blush deepened, and she gave them a wicked grin. "But that's not the point."

Stella and AJ laughed.

"I think it's a marvelous gift," AJ said. "It will show him how much it means to you that he's trying."

"Yeah, guys like that as much as women." Stella glanced out the window. "Speak of the devil. Isn't that Finn and Ethan leaving the general store?"

The women leaned over to stare out the window. Finn and Ethan juggled large bags in both hands as they hurried down the street before disappearing into the crowd of shoppers.

"What do you think were in those bags?" Maire asked, still watching the crowd.

"Adam wasn't with them. But he might have left earlier and we didn't notice," AJ said.

"Or Madelyn might have lured him away." Stella shoved three origami shapes into her purse. "That would have been awkward if we ran into them at the store."

"Maybe they were buying something for Helen. Or us." Maire tucked her napkin in the empty teacup.

"They were probably buying something for Adam's barbecue," Stella suggested, and they all laughed. Adam's devotion to his home barbecue was legendary.

"He was complaining about the grill last night. Not up to his standards." AJ had laughed at the time. Her brother had been bemoaning to Finn and Ethan the difficulties of working with an inferior grill. Adam cooked everything on the grill, and his barbecue was top of the line. It was only a matter of time before he'd said something about the old barbecue they'd borrowed here.

The women waited another five minutes before running over to the general store.

"Okay," AJ dropped several bundles of rope in the cart. "Their rope selection wasn't the best, but I think these will do. I'll have to tie some of them together."

"I found a backpack. Will these work?" Stella handed one of

three flashlights to AJ before she added the other two to their stash.

AJ read the label. "LED. That's good. And the top can be pulled up to make it more like a lantern. Oh, and it has two hooks. These are perfect." She dropped it in the cart with the others.

"Are these what you wanted? The manager said these are the only type they have. There's a climbing store a town over." Maire held out three different sizes of carabiners.

AJ ran her fingers over them, then tried to bend them. "They'll support our weight, but we'll need several. Did they have more of these?"

Maire nodded and led them to the display.

AJ grabbed several of each size. "I want to see if they have metal stakes."

"I need to grab something, too." Stella turned back the way they'd come. "I'll meet you at the register."

Maire followed AJ to the hardware section. "What are the stakes for?"

"Securing the line to the rock wall. From what I remembered, it's not entirely rock, so I only need a small hammer and some good stakes and we should be within safety limits."

"If we need to do any of this at all." Maire sounded discouraged.

"Sebastian might have left everything for you in his office. We'll know tomorrow."

"Maybe. But after everything that happened with the book and the stones, he was even more adamant about keeping everything apart. My greatest fear is we'll be left with a larger mystery than what we started with."

AJ found one selection of stakes, and after weighing them in her hands, she grabbed several and added the smallest hammer she could find. "And you're worried with how obsessive you've gotten just to see the journal that you'll be dragged deeper in." AJ turned to Maire. "That you'll want to go back."

Maire stared at the shelves rather than at AJ. When she finally glanced up, AJ winced at the tears shining in her eyes. "I struggle every day with who I am. Who I was meant to be. I love being here with you and my brother." She straightened and lifted her chin. "I think I've acclimated well to this time period."

AJ grinned. "You have." Then her grin faded. "But you need a purpose."

Maire nodded.

"What would that be if you went back?"

"That's the rub, isn't it? I'd want to be a scholar so I could research history."

"So basically, someone like Gallagher."

Maire looked sheepish. "I hadn't thought of it like that. But yes."

"But nothing exists like that in your time period. And there aren't women scholars in your time period. Or at least, they're quite rare."

"Ethan said as much."

"The way I see it, for once, time is on our side. Let's see what we find in Sebastian's lair, then enjoy the rest of the holidays. I know it's been a few months since you've been here, but so many other options have opened up. Just give it a little more time before you make a decision."

Maire grabbed her hand. "I promise."

They met Stella at the register. After checking out, they stepped to the side before exiting to stuff everything into the backpack.

"Are you planning on taking this all back home with you?" Stella asked as she shoved torn off labels and price tags into the shopping bag.

"Whatever we're not taking back with us we're giving to the monastery. If they can't use the items, they'll know who can."

AJ pushed through the door and almost tripped when it was opened at the same time by someone else. She glanced up and froze. "Finn." His large grin got her heart pumping again, but a flash in his gaze told her he was suspicious.

"Fancy meeting you here." Finn stepped aside. "Is there anything you need help carrying."

"Thank you, brother, but we're fine. What are you doing here?"

"Adam needed a new brush and tongs for the grill."

The women grinned at each other.

"The ones we already have aren't good enough?" AJ asked.

Finn held his grin and shrugged. "Something about the bristles. You know how he is."

AJ had to hand it to him. If they were up to something, Finn was a master at subterfuge. She'd learned that the hard way.

"Well, I got what I needed." Stella held up a box of stomach aids. Thank the heavens that woman was just as quick of wit as Finn.

"Don't let us keep you, brother. We have other stops to make before Helen wants us back for happy hour." Maire pushed past them, carrying the backpack low, but Finn glanced down. AJ had no doubt he'd seen it.

"See you soon." Finn pulled AJ close for a quick kiss. Then he whispered in her ear. "I love you."

She couldn't help it. She squeezed his ass. "Me too." Then raced to catch up with Stella and Maire.

When they reached the antique store, AJ stopped. "I need to run in and grab something. Meet you at the car."

Stella and Maire waved and kept going. No one wanted to run into Adam or Ethan. The last thing they needed was someone questioning the backpack.

13

After spending the morning and early afternoon playing board games, everyone filled the three rental cars and headed for the monastery. Sister Patrice arranged for a private tour of the Cider House with an accompanied meal. By the time they finished, Gallagher and team would be gone for the day.

The group was quiet as Finn drove the rental car into the monastery parking lot. The joyful atmosphere from the villa, where everyone had laughed and shared highlights of their trip, had faded into quiet reflection the minute they got in the vehicle. The fact Stella hadn't uttered a word on the drive spoke volumes to AJ. By the time they stepped out to the waning afternoon, the air seemed charged with a mixture of expectation and anxiety.

Adam opened the door for the kids then walked over to AJ. "Mom will take Madelyn and the kids back to the villa after we eat."

AJ glanced at Emory. "And the professor?"

Adam waved at Emory, who whispered something to their mother before joining them.

"They'll be ready to start the tour in about ten minutes." Emory clasped his hands and gave AJ a grave look. "I walk a fine line between this family and my friend. I've listened to Gallagher's position, and Brother Lucius gave me a private tour of the monastery, which included a lengthy history lesson." He turned to gaze at the monastery. His chest heaved with a long breath. "I can't tell you what it's like, being a historian, to stand in a building alive with its own history. To talk with people who have spent their life preserving it." He pushed his glasses up then stuck his hands in his pockets. "I'm here to learn, not to take sides. To explore." He gave AJ an earnest look. "I would never have this opportunity without you and your friends. And I appreciate Finn's offer to join you this evening. I promise to be discreet."

"Of course, you will." Stella joined them and put an arm through his. "You've been with us since the beginning."

AJ smiled at Stella's reverence for the professor. No matter how many times she heard stories about Adam and Stella's week of turmoil, her heart swelled with how they'd put away their differences to search for her. It meant the world to her and had healed the long rift with her brother, one neither of them could remember starting. Yet, when Adam shared stories of Stella fawning over the professor, she couldn't understand the draw until she'd met Emory.

When people first met Stella, who could be loud and cheeky at the best of times, they didn't consider her intelligence. They didn't see the woman who'd become the youngest broker in Baywood and built the top real estate business in the county. A one-woman business. They didn't know how often she read or explored the internet whenever a subject came up she wasn't familiar with. And she never felt the need to show off her smarts, so she was rarely recognized for it. When Emory acknowledged it the first time he'd met her, he'd won a fan for life.

"I was hoping you'd shared the tour with me today and let Helen hang with Adam and his family." Stella gave him her sad, puppy dog gaze, and he laughed as he patted her hand.

"I've been wondering when the two of us would have some time together. Let's get in line so we can make friends with the cider maker. We might sneak in an extra taste or two." The professor nodded at AJ and Adam as the two strode off toward the Cider House where last-minute customers were leaving.

Adam shook his head. "We've collected quite the group."

AJ took Adam's arm and steered him toward his family. "Do you remember the holidays last year?"

He grunted. "You came by Mom's for an early Christmas Eve dinner then raced out like your hair was on fire. If I remember it correctly, you and Stella rented a beach house down the coast and drank through the holiday."

AJ nudged him. "We didn't drink through the entire weekend. I was thinking more about how scattered we'd become. Now we have twice as many in our family. When we get home, we'll be even larger when we celebrate the new year with the Jackson's brood."

"And to think of what brought us all to this point."

She glanced over to where Finn stood with Ethan and Maire. Finn rubbed his sister's back, and Maire smiled at something Ethan said. "All because of the stones."

"It can make you crazy thinking about it. What do you think we'll find in Sebastian's library?"

AJ considered that. She'd thought of nothing else the last couple of days. The evening before, after everyone had gone to bed, she'd grabbed a bottle of wine and Finn, Ethan, and Maire had joined her in front of the fire as they discussed that same question. As the wine flowed, the answers became silly, but they all knew one thing to be true. There would be more journals, and as evident in the journal Gallagher had preserved under glass, Sebastian left cryptic notes for Maire. It might have just been an old man unable to let go of his memories from their time at the monastery, or missing the slip of an Irish woman who'd become his student and eventually surpassed her teacher. What no one wanted to consider, so they never mentioned it, was whether Sebastian had discovered something alarming that now lay buried under two hundred years of history. New information about the stones that might reach out and call them back.

The question of Maire's future still hadn't been written. AJ shook herself from her reverie when Adam squeezed her arm.

"Sorry, but that's a bit of a loaded question. There will be journals. We all feel positive about that."

"So, what has you so worried?"

She gave him a quick glance, unable to hold his gaze. She turned toward the rock wall that looked over the bay. She couldn't see the water, only the gray skies above it, and the cool breeze wrapped around her, forcing her to draw her jacket closer. "What cryptic message Sebastian left for Maire."

B rother Desmond met the group at the side door to the monastery after Helen and Madelyn said their good-byes and took off with the kids. The monk was all smiles through the introductions.

"Professor Gallagher and the rest of his staff left thirty minutes ago. We'll stop by the kitchen to get Sister Patrice then go down to the tunnels." Desmond was a thin man, maybe a couple of years younger than AJ, with shaggy black hair that he kept pushing behind his ears. He wore the traditional robes, the pockets bulging with who knew what, and pink sneakers which made AJ smile. "Brother Lucius will meet us there."

"I thought Brother Lucius had other plans." Finn shook the young monk's hand and followed him into the monastery.

Desmond's nods were like rapid fire. "He found someone else to take over his duties. This was a lifelong opportunity he couldn't pass up."

"Told you, so." Stella was back to hanging on Emory's arm.

"Not too much of a surprise, considering his hospitality at opening the basement to us." Ethan guided Maire through the hallway as the group marched to the kitchen.

Sister Patrice wasn't in the kitchen. She was waiting at the basement door, apparently as eager as the rest of them. When she saw them approach, she unlocked the door and opened it.

AJ's heart raced as she peered down the stairs. This was different than preparing to go down these same stairs yesterday. This was the real deal this time, and the thought made her stomach flip. She gripped Finn's hand, and he held it tightly as they followed Ethan and Maire down the stairs. The group turned right and then left before coming across Brother Lucius sitting on a stool next to a door at the end of a hall.

Brother Desmond opened the door, and AJ peeked over Maire's shoulder, but there was nothing but dark stone walls. A shiver went through her—the second staircase.

Desmond picked up an LED lantern, this one much larger than the ones the women had bought. "There are two more lanterns here. Pass them out so someone in the middle and at the end have one. That should provide enough light, but we'll move slowly. This part of the tunnels hasn't been remodeled, but we use the available space for storage."

He led them down the rough-hewn stairs and past two rooms. "You can see the yellow caution tape. Several yards further is where the ceiling collapsed. Decades ago, they tried to open the walls between rooms, but it destabilized this section of tunnels. The entire area requires reinforcement. The brothers never had a reason for further exploration down here. Not until the archaeologists arrived. We've recently started a construction fund to reopen the collapsed tunnel so we can see what else is down here."

"Do you have access to the third level?" Ethan asked.

Desmond nodded. "But it was determined the rest of the tunnels should be considered unsafe until we have them certified by an engineer which will be part of the larger project. We hope to start in five years." He turned the lantern toward an alcove several feet from the yellow tape. "The only item of historical value is this old statue, but Professor Gallagher determined that, other than an interesting story of why it was there, it held no other value."

AJ felt her bicep being squeezed and glanced over to find Maire clutching her arm as she stared at the tall statue.

It was a soldier in ancient armor carved from soft stone. Age had rounded its once sharp edges, yet two hundred years hadn't changed her memories of it. The LED lit up the statue and the filigree decor behind it, but even modern-day lighting couldn't uncover the hidden door to Sebastian's library or the secret viewing window that Sebastian used to check the hall before leaving the room.

"Why are we all staring at a statue? Is it valuable?" Stella pushed AJ to the side so she could see it. Then backed away to let Emory look.

"It's the entrance to Sebastian's library." Ethan put an arm around Maire. "This is it. Are you ready?"

Everyone's gaze turned to Maire, and the air stirred with anticipation. Maybe AJ was the only one feeling it, but based on the other's expressions with their mouths opened in wonder or their eyes wide with excitement, there wasn't a doubt everyone understood how incredible this was. But when she glanced at Finn and Ethan, she noted their acceptance that this step would change things. The question was, to what degree?

She turned to her friend. This was the moment that would lay out Maire's future. She felt it to her bones, and she wiped away the moisture at her eyes, and held her breath.

Maire, her expression bright and hopeful, took a deep breath and let out a low sigh before stepping to the statue. She reached behind it and the sound of rock scraping on rock pierced the tunnel. The monks, Stella, and Adam held their hands to their ears. The sound was definitely louder than she remembered.

"The shift from the cave-in must have impacted the door." Finn pulled Maire back so he could enter first. "Let me make sure it's safe first."

Ethan held onto her arm, but AJ doubted Maire was aware. Her focus was trained on her brother as she shifted from foot to foot. The light from the LED moved around the room, stopping for a minute before moving again.

Finn stepped out and handed Maire the lantern. His gaze sparkled within its illumination and a wide grin filled his face. "It's all yours, sister."

Maire nodded as she took the lantern and stepped into the room. She took two steps then stopped.

Ethan turned and nodded to AJ. "You next."

AJ's feet stuck to the floor, but she dragged a hesitant step then nudged Maire to move her farther into the room. Both women turned slowly as Maire held up the lantern while they scanned the room.

Maire held a hand to her mouth. "My God, AJ. It's like we never left."

She was right. If the lighting was different, about half as bright, not so sharp, and tinged with yellow, AJ would expect Sebastian to walk in at any moment. Tremors ran through her, and she crossed her arms. It was chilly in the room, but she didn't think her shakes were from the cold.

Maire immediately walked to his workstation where he'd mixed his potions and teas. She picked up pieces—a spoon, a cup, a quill, and an open inkpot long gone dry. She organized as she went, probably out of habit.

AJ was pushed aside as others entered, first Finn and then Ethan, followed by six others until everyone was shoulder to shoulder in the limited space. With the additional lanterns, the room was too bright, and Sister Patrice turned one off as if reading her mind. Multiple oil lanterns hung from hooks on the wall. The same wooden table where Maire hunched for days over *The Book of Stones* was surrounded by six high-backed chairs, those being an upgrade from what AJ remembered. Half the group dragged the chairs out to sit while the rest wandered the room. The table was covered with piles of books and loose papers. Another quill, this inkpot closed, lay next to another lamp. Three walls were lined with overstuffed bookcases. The fourth wall was filled with Sebastian's workstation and a side table where an old clay teapot, several mugs, and a warmer sat.

Maire turned from the workstation and leaned over the table, scanning the books. She carefully turned pages on the one by the inkpot. "This looks to be his last journal." She read the last few pages. "His last entries are about his latest procurement. It appears he'd been searching for artifacts that had been taken from the monastery during the Terror."

"You can read it?" Stella leaned over from where she sat, keeping her voice low.

Maire nodded and smiled. "It's in French. And I've read many of his journals."

"Why are you smiling?" Finn usually remained quiet on his visits to the monastery. AJ hadn't given it much consideration, but maybe she should have. He hadn't said much about it one way or another, though he usually found a way to stay away. And with Emory always at the monastery, Finn used the excuse of keeping her mom company. The two got along great, so AJ hadn't thought anything of it, but maybe the memories of his time here was just as hard on him, even if he never let his smile slip.

"Sebastian was using the proceeds from the smuggling to purchase the artifacts."

"Smart man." Ethan watched Maire, his eyes narrowed as he studied her. "Anything at his workstation?"

She shook her head. "No. Just old herbs and teas. All of his paperwork is on the table." She leaned in closer and whispered, "That was normal. Even when he took notes on his potions, he didn't want any paper getting damaged."

AJ glanced at Patrice, but she had moved to one of the bookcases.

Soon, everyone became immersed in seeing what treasures Sebastian might have left behind. Emory sat at the table, reading Sebastian's last journal, while Brother Desmond pulled out a notebook. He studied a label from a jar of tea, scribbled something down, then moved on to the next, repeating the task. Maybe he was an herbalist, or maybe he was doing it for Brother Lucius, who seemed to be one of the monastery's gardeners.

Maire's first stop was the bookcase where Sebastian had originally hid a portion of *The Book of Stones*. Maire's shoulders slumped when she pulled back the books to search behind them. She leaned against the case and scanned the other bookcases, which had to be difficult with everyone circulating around them. Her gaze turned back to the workstation, and she gave the group a quick glance before tiptoeing to it and running her hands along the left side. A door popped open, and she turned, catching AJ watching her. AJ nodded and, keeping her eyes on the rest of the group, she stood to find something of interest on the workstation that would block the others' view of Maire.

A bare minute passed before Maire turned, smoothing out her coat after stuffing something in its pocket.

"What did you find?" AJ's gaze stayed on the others, but everyone was busy with their own pursuits. Most were reviewing the books, practicing great care when opening one. Stella found a cupboard filled with gadgets that she was picking through with Brother Desmond. Then she noticed Ethan and Finn in the corner, their chairs together as they whispered, but their gazes were locked on her and Maire.

Maire's gaze darted around the room, resting on Brother Lucius and Sister Patrice, who were reading a large tome the monk held, but she took a step closer to AJ. "Sebastian left me one of his journals." Her voice was low, and her eyes sparkled with excitement.

"How do you know it was meant for you?"

"My initials are on the inside cover and the entire journal is written in Celtic. He only used French in his journals."

AJ's heart beat louder. What did that mean? She slowed her breathing. He just wanted to leave her some final thoughts in case she didn't return before he died, and he wrote in Celtic because he probably mentioned time travel. But the prickly tightness in her stomach told her something different. She ignored it all, deciding to worry once they could talk freely.

Maire left her side to join Brother Lucius and Sister Patrice, just as Emory shouted out, "Here. I found more of Sebastian's journals."

Everyone rushed to see. All except Maire. The itchy twinge

in AJ's belly turned to stone. She turned to the workstation and gripped its edge until her fingers ached. Foreboding crushed her as her spidey senses tingled. She wanted to leave France. Right now. She didn't want to see what she suspected waited for them on the other side of the iron door.

14

After dinner, and after most had gone to bed, AJ, Finn, Stella, and Ethan huddled around the fireplace in the living room. Adam had wanted to stay, but it was better to leave with Madelyn, otherwise, there would be questions. Finn promised to catch him up in the morning.

AJ gripped her wine-glass as she stared past the coffee table. A bottle of Irish whiskey and one of wine marred a clear view of the fire until everything else blurred except a single flame.

Finn clasped her hand, breaking the spell. He sipped his whiskey, giving her a questioning look before returning to small talk with the others.

Maire had holed up in the bedroom she shared with Ethan so she could read Sebastian's journal in peace. She'd said little on their drive back from the monastery, having read only enough to know the journal was meant for her. Once back at the villa, she became animated throughout dinner and remained so as they played board games afterward. It wasn't until the kids were sent to bed and others eventually followed that she expressed her desire for privacy.

That had been an hour ago.

"I'm sure it won't be much longer." Ethan refilled his glass, and when Finn nodded, topped off his, too.

Another thirty minutes dragged by with discussions of how to fill the remaining days of their trip. The following day was Christmas Eve, and everyone wanted to stay close and prepare a large dinner celebration since they would all be traveling to the countryside on Christmas Day with dreams of returning to the villa for leftovers. After that, they would have two more days in France before leaving for home.

A clatter of dishes in the kitchen made everyone turn their heads. Maybe Helen couldn't sleep and needed a snack. Or Madelyn was getting something for the kids. Her gaze widened when Maire strolled in with a tray, which she waited to set on the coffee table while everyone scrambled to move bottles and glasses.

The tray held a plate of melting brie covered with raspberry sauce and surrounded by flaky crackers. Maire had even taken the time to garnish it with grapes. She handed the plates to Stella, who passed them around accompanied with a butter knife and napkin.

"What's the occasion?" Ethan massaged Maire's neck after she sat next to him. "You've been bent over that book for hours."

"Are we celebrating something?" Finn poured another round of whiskey but pushed his glass aside in favor of the cheese treat.

"Don't start, brother." Maire cut a slice of brie and placed it on her plate followed by a handful of crackers. She settled back on the couch, her thigh touching Ethan's. She ate two crackers, chewing slowly, forcing the others to grab a plate if they didn't want to sit in silence until she was ready to speak.

Stella popped up and grabbed the empty wine bottle. "I'll

grab another selection. Thank God we're in France." She continued to mumble on her way to the kitchen. AJ understood Stella's jitters. As important as it was for Maire to have final words from Sebastian, the fact the journal was hidden could only spell trouble.

Stella returned quickly, as if she knew something important was ready to be revealed.

"How did you know where to find the journal?" AJ had expected Maire to check the bookshelf where Sebastian had hidden *The Book of Stones*, but the hidden drawer was another matter. "You must have known about the drawer before."

Maire nodded as she nibbled a cracker. She wiped the crumbs from her lips. "Sebastian has secret rooms, doors, and drawers everywhere. Monks before him built most of them, their location handed down through stories to younger monks. Very little was ever written down, just like the druids. But Sebastian worried about the decrease of monks after the Terror, so he began making notes about the secret passages and various artifacts. Everything was written in Celtic and other ancient languages to make it difficult to find them. But he didn't want the artifacts lost forever."

"Are those the ledgers Gallagher has?" Ethan took the wine bottle from Stella and finished filling glasses.

"No. But from what Desmond told me, he's confirmed they're ship manifests from the smuggling operation." She grinned at Finn. "I imagine there are several lines of cargo from the *Daphne Marie*."

"From what Jamie shared with me, I have no doubt." Finn's return smile didn't quite meet his eyes, and he turned his gaze to the fire. A twang pinched AJ's heart. He had a new sailboat. A shiny, modern one with all the bells and whistles. But his heart would forever be with the first *Daphne*, and even with the short time she'd spent on the ship, it would always hold a special place for her. It wasn't difficult to imagine how deeply Finn missed her.

"I think Desmond will find everything he needs in Sebastian's library." Maire set her plate down and brushed off her flowing skirt. "The secret drawer in his workstation isn't very big. Almost the perfect size for one journal. He would drop notes to me in the drawer anytime he remembered something and I wasn't there. I would leave him a few. I'd hoped *The Book of Stones* was where he'd last put it but, after reading this journal, I understand why it isn't."

Stella had taken a stack of napkins and was busy making origami fish, adding her own unique style to them. She'd made a few different animal figures to show Charlotte, who'd decided in no uncertain terms that the fish were her favorite. "Let's just get to it. Is it still around?"

Maire hesitated, then shook her head. "After Reginald and Dugan returned, Sebastian was concerned others knew of the Book. He kept it in its four pieces, and after writing what a difficult decision it had been, he sent them to four trustworthy people."

"And who are these four people? Does the journal mention them?" Finn's attention remained on his sister.

Maire lowered her head. "No."

"It was a fairly full journal from what I saw." Ethan turned in his seat so he could face her. "There must have been more."

AJ didn't sense he didn't believe her, but Finn's gaze had narrowed. He knew Maire better than anyone, but if AJ had caught her slight behavior tells, Ethan would pick up on it as well. It wasn't that she was lying, Maire didn't do that. But she was excellent in talking her way around questions.

Maire slid to the edge of the sofa and placed the empty

plates in a stack. "He told me what was in each of the four sections. Which pieces gave which information about the stones and the torc. He didn't mention where he put *The Mórdha Stone Grimoire*." When Stella gave her a puzzled look, Maire added, "The druid's book."

"Ah." Stella nodded then sipped her wine before returning to her fish.

"What about the stones and torc themselves?" AJ glanced at the group. *The Book of Stones* did little good without the primary elements of time travel. "Are they still hidden within the monastery?"

"If they are, they can stay hidden." Stella's tone brooked no argument. "Why would we want them where someone could find them? Unless you think Gallagher could find them. But without the Book, who cares?"

"What date was the journal written?" Finn asked.

"Yes. That should have been our first thought. We have no idea when any of this happened," Ethan mused.

Maire frowned. "I'm afraid the journal isn't dated."

"Just like there being no actual record of his death," AJ added.

Finn tapped his glass then finished off the whiskey. "That puts a wrinkle in things, but we still need to know as much as we can. Maybe something will standout. So, were the stones and torc in the monastery according to the journal?"

Maire shrugged. "He did say the stones and torc were still well hidden. If I read it correctly, he decided to keep the stones and torc together. As long as the Book was spread far and wide, he thought they would be safe."

AJ snorted. "When you and I first met him, he'd been appalled when I suggested burning the Book. But if they've been scattered, it's almost the same thing."

"Not in Sebastian's eyes." Maire understood the monk like no other. But AJ wasn't able to keep up with what might be the truth versus what Maire wasn't saying. It didn't seem to bother her friend because she ignored AJ's grunts. "As long as the pages exist in the world, even if parted for mankind's benefit, he's done his job. He understood as well as we did how dangerous the stones would be in the wrong hands, assuming anyone knew what to do with them." She patted Ethan's knee. "There were several pages of other interesting objects he'd uncovered. Much of the journal is about his days at the monastery." She stood and picked up the tray. "Well, I don't know about you, but it's been a long, stressful day. Since we have big evening plans tomorrow, I thought us girls could do some last-minute Christmas shopping in the morning."

Finn and Ethan glanced at each other. But whether they thought Maire's suggestion strange for them to be on their own, or they had their own plans, AJ couldn't tell.

"I think that's a great idea." Stella jumped up. "I saw something for Madelyn, and I'd like to see if the store still has it." She picked up the half-empty wine bottle and followed Maire to the kitchen.

After saying goodnight, Ethan followed them.

Finn took AJ's hand and led her the opposite way to their room. "You three don't have something planned, do you?"

AJ put an arm around his waist and gave him a gentle hug. "Our focus has been getting to Sebastian's library, and now we've done that." She increased her pace. "I don't know about you, but I could use a warm bath before bed. It would be a shame to waste such a large tub."

If Finn had any more thoughts about the journal, the stones, or the Book, AJ didn't hear another word about it the rest of the evening.

The next morning, after a filling meal of Helen's crepes and Ethan's surprise egg scramble, Stella drove AJ and Maire back to the monastery. She slid into a parking spot directly in front of the Cider House.

"I said close to the Cider House, not in front of it." AJ got out of the car and pulled her backpack from the back. Sometimes Stella was just too literal.

"In an hour, the lot will be full. If someone comes looking for us, the front row will be the last place they look."

"That's smart." Maire began walking toward the monastery, not waiting for the others to join in.

AJ grunted.

Stella, being the better sport, just patted AJ on the back before following Maire.

AJ couldn't help but smile. It wasn't really a game, but somehow, over the last few months with Maire, Stella had begun paying attention to which of them noted her quick wit. She couldn't blame Stella. As she had told her friend earlier that week, she was smart even if people didn't see it right away. Having another intelligent woman like Maire around, Stella felt the need to let her own brains show. And AJ thought it was a good look for her.

She followed the women across the parking lot and glanced at the monastery, hoping there wasn't anyone out who might recognize them. Gallagher and his team would have the day off, and from what she'd heard Sister Patrice say, the monks would be at holiday vigils most of the day. They should be safe from curious eyes.

The sky was overcast and a light wind blowing in from the coast forced her to zip up her jacket. When they reached the rusty iron stairs, AJ didn't doddle. She laid out the rope and three harnesses she'd made on the drive over. After giving each harness a once-over, she made Stella and Maire step into one, which AJ then checked for snugness before pulling on her own. Next, she did a quick check of the carabiners, which she had connected to a small rope ring that she tied to one of her belt loops. They swung like a heavy set of keys. She removed four of them and connected two carabiners to each of the other harnesses. The last items she retrieved were the hammer and stakes which had been stuffed into a zippered bag she'd repurposed from her luggage. She pulled on gloves, then stepped to the edge of the first step, bouncing on it while she observed the iron nails that had been driven into the rock.

"Do you have to bounce?" Stella stood behind her, fussing with her harness. "Maybe you should just hook us up to a rope and lower us down from the other side."

AJ tied the end of the rope to the stair frame near the highest iron bolt. She tugged hard on it. "This anchor is stronger than any I can drive in. It's sturdy enough to hold our weight should the stairs fail."

"Explain exactly what we need to do?" Maire watched every motion AJ made as if committing it to memory.

"I'll hook the two carabiners on your harness to the rope. The rope will be doubled. One line will be connected to the stakes, you'll be hooked onto the other. All you have to do is take each step slowly, make sure your full weight is on a step before taking the next step. Remember, slow and steady."

She took a moment to observe Maire's wrinkled brow and Stella's wide eyes. "Look. The staircase may jiggle a bit. But going slow, you'll barely feel it. If I find anything that makes this riskier than I feel comfortable with, I'll come back up, and we'll do it the hard way." She waited for head nods then continued, "Once

I'm at the ledge, I'll call up for the next person. Do you have your lock picks?"

Stella patted her jacket pocket. "Right here."

"Okay, you'll go after me so you can start on the lock while Maire comes down."

Maire glanced at Stella, whose eyes were wide as she licked her lips. "Is there a problem?"

It took a second before Stella realized Maire was talking to her. She shook her head. "Just a small issue with heights."

Maire turned to AJ with a helpless shrug.

AJ nodded and touched Stella's shoulder. "That's okay. If you get part way down and can't go any farther, just let us know. The stairs are safe for more than one person, I'm just being careful. Maire can come down and help you along."

Stella nodded. "I'll be fine."

With that, AJ wasted no time in grabbing the pile of rope she'd tied on and ventured down the first step. Twenty minutes later, she called up, "The line's secure. Watch the fifth step. It's looser than the others, but it will still hold you."

AJ waited at the bottom step and saw a tug on the rope that told her Stella was on her way down. She smiled at the gulls that flew close but kept her eyes on the rope. It slackened for a couple of minutes, tightened, and then someone screamed.

"Stella?" AJ yelled, her heart in her throat. Maire's yell was even louder, and AJ focused on the rope for signs of tension. Tiny pebbles rolled down the steps. "Stella, talk to me right now." Her voice had risen an octave.

"Yeah, sorry. Found the fifth step. I guess I miscounted." Stella's voice was calm, and AJ's breath rushed out of her.

Moments later, Stella's mumbling reached AJ before she saw her round a slight curve. She couldn't tell what Stella was saying but ventured a guess it was a combination of swear words and prayer.

Stella was pale when she reached the bottom, her face shiny with perspiration, but her intense scowl flipped to a huge smile when her feet landed on the ledge. "Made it. That was easy."

AJ couldn't decide whether to hug her or swat her, so she just snorted. "I guess I should have spray painted a huge X on the fifth step as a reminder."

It was meant as sarcasm, but Stella ignored it. "That would have helped."

AJ could have sworn she saw Stella grin as she made a circle to take in the ledge. She was already opening her pocket to retrieve her lock pick set as she strode toward the iron door, so AJ decided against any witty comeback. Not that she had one prepared.

"Can I come down now?"

AJ turned her attention back to the stairs. "Yeah, ready down here."

Maire was down in half the time it took Stella, her eyes sparkling. "I think I understand why you climb. That was exhilarating, and all I did was walk down rusty stairs."

AJ grinned. "Maybe you should take a class. I would love a climbing partner."

"Don't tempt me."

Maire glanced over AJ's shoulder, and she turned to see what Maire was looking at. Stella stood a few feet from the iron door, the padlock swinging from her finger.

"Really? All ready?" AJ could only stare.

Stella shrugged. "I've got skills."

AJ grunted, stuffed the harnesses in the backpack, and tossed it to Stella. When she reached the iron door and grabbed the handle, it wouldn't budge. It took all three of them prying at the door while straining their muscles before they wrenched it open. AJ could only assume the door hadn't been used enough to combat the decades of salty spray and fierce winter storms.

Once the door was open, the three stared into the darkness. AJ wiped away the cobwebs that had formed from abandonment. She stepped inside and took several steps before calling back, "Get the lanterns."

15

Finn, Ethan, and Adam stood on the back patio of the villa, staring at a sketch that lay on the table.

"I think we should start here, then move along the front." Adam ran his finger down a line. "Ethan and I can tackle that. Finn, you start on the inside. I've listed out each step."

Ethan and Finn stared at the sketch then at each other.

"Are you sure about this?" Ethan asked.

Finn reviewed the list. It seemed simple enough, although he was having a hard time seeing how everything came together. "Adam is the expert in this, so I don't see another option." He checked his watch. "The women should be gone for several hours." He peered through the windows into the villa. "Where are Helen and Madelyn?"

"They're with the kids on one of their own projects. They were talking about running into town as well, so I thought we could start as soon as they leave. They'll have the kids with them." Adam folded the sketch and tucked it in his pocket.

"Did anything seem off with Maire and AJ this morning?" Ethan dropped into a chair and stared out to the Channel. He was becoming as moody as Maire.

Adam laughed. "You mean with all that bath time before shopping? I think even Mom thought it was odd."

Finn sat and drank the cooling coffee. "They've been up to something for days. I thought it would end after finding Sebastian's library. And from what Maire told us of this secret journal, it sounded like there wasn't anything more to dwell on."

Ethan scratched his head. "Maire did seem satisfied with it, elated actually. I don't know. It just seems like it was too quick of a mood shift."

Finn had thought the same thing at first. It wasn't just Maire with the swift change of behavior, but AJ, too. They had originally seemed glum after discovering what was in the journal, but everything was sunshine and good tides this morning. His only disappointment had been AJ kicking him out of the bathroom when he wanted to share the bath with her. He slammed the mug on the table.

"They're still up to something." Finn glanced at the other men. "I admit, their good mood could be nothing more than moving past their questions about Sebastian. Nothing was overly suspicious until that damn bath."

"Do you think Maire lied about what was in the journal?" Ethan's expression reflected his doubt.

"Lied?" Finn's smile wasn't his typical friendly one. "Maire is a manipulator. No. She didn't lie."

Ethan groaned. "But she didn't reveal the entire truth."

Adam shook his head, a frown forming small creases in his forehead. "After you gave me a debrief this morning, and seeing the women at breakfast, they convinced me."

Finn stood. "The three of them have spent too much time together." He turned to Adam. "How much of our plan can you put into play if we have to leave you alone for a bit?"

Adam sipped his coffee and stared at the porch ceiling before excitement lit his eyes. "I've been thinking about this all wrong. I'll enlist Helen and the kids. Madelyn will drink wine and direct from the sidelines. They love this stuff. It will be more of a family adventure. But where are you two going?"

Ethan glanced at Finn. "I think trying to find them in town would be difficult."

"Aye. We only need to make a trip to the monastery. If they're not there, then we come back and help Adam."

Thirty minutes later, Finn drove into the lot for Cider House customers and scanned the cars. There were more here than he'd expected on Christmas Eve.

"Is this the last-minute shopping crowd Stella mentioned?" Ethan stared out the front window, his head pivoting as he scanned the lot.

Finn shrugged. "Or a family tradition to stop in."

"And if the women spot us?

Finn grinned. "We're stopping by for a cider. Why bother going to Guerin's with the Cider House so close?

"There." Ethan pointed to a small SUV, and after glancing at the license plate, Finn agreed.

The car was right in front of the Cider House, which could have been their luck in finding someone leaving, or they'd gotten here before the building opened.

He drove past and searched for their own parking spot four lanes away. They walked back to the rental car, and Finn felt the hood. "It's cold."

"Those three at a drinking establishment?" Ethan shook his head, but there was a crease of worry over his brows.

"Let's go in and check." Finn led the way and stared at the crowd. There was a line for the mill tour, others pushed their way in and out of the gift shop, and the rest filled the tables, partaking of the house cider while nibbling what Stella called tapas.

"I don't see them." Ethan stood on tiptoes to get a better look.

"Let's split up and do a search, then meet back here."

Finn moved to the left, taking his time, smiling and nodding to other customers while he searched for any sign of the women. After making a small half circle, he met Ethan at the entrance, shook his head, and kept walking until he reached the women's SUV. He stared at the monastery.

Ethan fell in next to him and followed his gaze. "You think they're meeting with Sister Patrice or Brother Desmond?"

Finn checked his watch. "Not with holiday vigils. From what Emory said, the monastery will be all but buttoned up until the day after Christmas. Even Gallagher and his crew will be gone until then."

"So where the devil are they?"

Finn considered it. He groaned. He'd thought he and AJ had gotten past their secrets. Trouble was, their time jump, which should have scared them enough to never mention the stones again, had only spurred a wicked adventurous streak in AJ. If they were still living in 1804, that might be okay. But these times were more precarious when the police were more organized.

"What?" Ethan scanned the area before turning back to Finn.

"I have one idea. Follow me." Finn took off and headed toward the front of the monastery. If he didn't feel like throttling AJ, he would have chuckled when he heard Ethan's responding curse when they walked past the entrance. He'd have it out with Maire as well. Hell, all three deserved a good thrashing once he caught up with them.

―――――――

AJ led the women through the tunnels. Other than the fancy LED lantern rather than the old oil type, time seemed to have stopped within the damp walls. She moved the flashlight around, checking for anything that might suggest instability but didn't see any crumbled dirt or pieces of rock. The packed ground was as smooth as she remembered it. Barring any unexpected cave-ins, it was a short walk to the smugglers meeting room where she'd once met up with the crew of the *Daphne*. She smiled at the memory. How scared she'd been, having arrived with Beckworth in tow, yet courageous at the same time. She'd kept her head and puzzled out a solution, and while not perfect, had ended well enough.

"I'm surprised Maire's idea of a texting while bathing worked." Stella was so close behind her, she was almost walking on her heels, as if AJ would disappear down a dark tunnel without her. "I knew there had to be more in the journal."

AJ paused to check on Maire, who was moving slowly even though she knew the tunnels as well as AJ did. "I thought I wouldn't make it on time. Finn insisted on sharing the bath."

Stella snorted. "We could have waited five minutes."

"Funny." AJ raised her light to see Maire, who laughed at Stella's remark. "Are you okay back there?"

"Yes. I was just thinking about the journal. Maybe we should have said something to Ethan and Finn."

AJ shook her head. "Weren't you the one that wanted to wait until we saw what Sebastian left in the meeting room?"

"It seemed right at the time. Now, I'm not sure."

"Well, that ship sailed." Stella bumped into AJ. "Sorry. Are we almost there?"

"Yes. And step back a few feet. You have your own lantern; you don't have to follow so close."

"I can't help it. I get claustrophobic."

"Shouldn't you have said something before now? You could have waited at the iron door." Maire was closer now, knowing they were almost there.

"And miss all this? This is the closest I'll get to living a small part of your adventure." Stella gave AJ distance as they continued until AJ stopped at a stone bench. Then Stella let out a guttural sigh. "Oh, good, a resting spot in the middle of a tunnel maze. Did they put this here for the terribly lost individuals?" She ran her lantern around the area. "No bones, so I assumed they eventually got out."

AJ laughed. "I thought the same thing when Sebastian stopped here." She reached for the stone motif then ran her hand down to the third stone and pushed in. A portion of the wall next to them pushed open with a rush of stale air.

"That is amazing. Just like Sebastian's library." Stella ran her flashlight along the ground and followed it up the wall. "You can barely see where it was joined."

"I don't know who made these secret walls and doors, but they were masterful."

"Can we discuss this inside?" Maire pushed past AJ and Stella and pried the door the rest of the way open.

AJ and Stella smiled at each other. Someone was in a hurry, but AJ couldn't blame Maire. Though she'd seemed fine all morning, smiling and joking with everyone at breakfast, she didn't fool AJ. They'd spent too much time in harrowing positions to not sense each other's emotions. She was only surprised Ethan and Finn hadn't picked up on it.

Once they were all inside, AJ flashed the light around the room. The same long table with twenty chairs. She could swear she heard the men talking as if they were here but couldn't be seen. Tears brimmed as she thought of Lando, Jamie, and Fitz. She shook her head and placed her lantern on the table. Stella placed hers next to it.

Maire kept hers to aid in her inspection of the walls. On her second circle around the room, she slowed as she approached a back corner. She ran the light up the wall to where a sconce once held an oil lamp. She tried turning the sconce, but it wouldn't budge.

"Here." She handed AJ the lantern. "Keep it on the sconce." She tried again, this time with both hands, but nothing happened.

"Could it be one of the other ones?" Stella asked.

Maire stepped back, hands on hips, and glanced down at the floor. "I don't think so."

"Let's try them anyway." AJ stepped to the closest one and gave it a turn both ways. Nothing.

When they'd all been tested, AJ studied the first sconce. "Maybe it's just stuck. It's been a couple hundred years if Sebastian was the last one to use it." She looked through the backpack Stella had placed on the dusty table and pulled out the hammer. "Let's give this a try."

After a couple light taps followed by a harder one, the sconce moved to the left.

Maire held her lantern toward the floor. "Once more."

AJ did as she was told, and a grating sound filled the room.

"Bingo." Maire dropped to her knees.

"Bingo? Have you been gambling?" Stella chided as she crouched next to Maire.

"Maire heard Finn use the word and now it seems to be her go-to word whenever a plan comes together." AJ leaned against another wall as she watched Maire flash the light into the hole. Her shoulders dropped as she reached in. Something was definitely in there.

When Maire stood, she held a familiar object. Another of Sebastian's journals.

Stella whistled. "Bingo was right."

The three sat at the table, and AJ slid the third lantern next to the other two to give Maire as much light as possible. Maire took her time reading the first couple of pages then scanned the rest.

"So, what did he say? Is it written in Celtic, too?" Stella leaned in, trying to get a look.

AJ waited her turn, as if it mattered. It would be in Celtic, and she wouldn't be able to read a word of it.

"Yes. He gives a brief summary at the beginning." She sat back, tears on her face as she smiled at them. "It's all here."

Stella gave AJ a worried glance.

"How do you know?" AJ said.

"Sebastian says it all in the first few pages. Who he sent the sections of book to, where the druid's book is, and where the torc and the rest of the stones are."

"He said all that in two pages?" Stella's brows were knit, and she frowned. She wasn't buying it any more than AJ was.

"He suggested it within the two pages. I'll have to read the rest and decipher Sebastian's code."

AJ groaned. "You mean he wrote it like the druids? In some form of Sebastian encryption?"

Maire nodded and gave AJ that look. That look that said she wanted to stay and read it.

"No. We can't stay. It's Christmas Eve. We have to go." AJ wasn't going to fall for Maire's begging. "Can't we take it with?"

They paused to consider, each in their own thoughts.

"Why don't we just photograph the pages and put the journal back?" Stella pulled out her phone. "I have enough battery and plenty of space. All my photos are backed up to the cloud."

Maire looked at her. "The cloud?"

"Let's not go there right now." AJ pulled out her own phone. "Maire, let's use your phone, but I don't know if it has the same backup as Stella's. Let's play it safe. We'll all take a picture of each page. That way we can make sure we have at least one clear picture of the writing."

The first few pages took longer than AJ wanted, but the three settled into a rhythm and completed their task within thirty minutes. Maire reviewed a few pictures on all the phones and nodded her approval.

Maire grinned, her eyes wide, her expression happier than AJ had seen in a while. "This was a grand idea, Stella." She ran her hand over the journal.

"You have Sebastian's other journal." AJ touched Maire's arm. "He'd be happy to know you have that one."

Maire wiped her eyes and put the journal back where she'd found it. AJ moved the sconce back in place, sealing the hiding place. They were packed up and exiting the room five minutes later. AJ gave one last look around before shutting the door with a finality that sent goosebumps down her arms. She shook off whatever premonition wanted head space, convincing herself it was nothing more than memories eager to see the light of day.

Maire took the lead back to the iron door, and once outside, all three leaned against the rock wall and breathed in the salty air as if they'd been trapped in the tunnels for days. Then they looked at each other and laughed until Stella stared at the staircase that waited for them.

"Okay, back the same way we came." AJ passed out the harnesses. After they were ready, AJ connected Maire's harness onto the line. After five minutes, AJ felt the strong tug on the line, and she turned to fasten Stella's harness.

"The cider is on me when we get to the top." Stella glanced toward the bay and shivered.

"Don't look down." AJ pushed a lock of Stella's hair away from her face since Stella's grip was tightly wrapped around the rope that followed the stairs up. "Claustrophobic and a fear of heights. How did I not know this?"

"Because we had a stable life until now. That's why." Stella's voice had risen an octave.

"The stairs are fine. Just one at a time, and remember that fifth step." She smiled and waited for Stella's reluctant nod. "And I think we're due more than one round."

Stella nodded again, a weak smile on her lips, and began her climb. When AJ felt the strong tug on the rope again, she glanced at the locked iron door, and like Maire, wished they had more time. The walk up was easy, the staircase still stable except for that one loose spot in the middle but strong enough to support her weight. When she got to the top, she expected Maire and Stella to be there, but all she found were their harnesses. Shaking her head at being left behind, she pulled up the rope, having tucked the stakes in their pouch as she removed them on her way up. Once the rope was folded and packed, she stuffed the harnesses in and followed the path back toward the monastery.

She only walked twenty yards before stopping. Maire and Stella waited for her, their expressions sheepish as they stood behind Finn and Ethan. Both men stood with their feet apart and their arms crossed over their chests like centurions with their prisoners.

Finn's expression was a mask of two moods warring with each other. His eyes were narrowed and flinty, and though his lips were pressed into a thin line, they quirked at the edges. She held back a smile, understanding his need to yell at her, even though he could barely hold his grin in check. They were pissed, but if she had to guess, they were only sorry they hadn't been able to go with them. And she regretted not including them in their adventure, even though she knew they would have put a stop to it.

"How did you know we were here?" she asked when she reached Finn.

"The rope tied to the staircase."

She nodded at his flat response and walked next to Maire and Stella as they followed the unspeaking men back to the cars. The women slid glances at each other but couldn't stop smiling. And AJ was fairly certain she caught Finn and Ethan with a grin of their own.

16

Finn walked the group back to the SUV the women had driven, opening a back passenger door while Ethan opened the other one. Stella jumped in first, then Maire quickly followed, climbing in the side where Finn waited. AJ walked toward Ethan and slid in. Finn dropped into the driver's seat and held out his hand until Stella tossed him the keys. The group remained silent as Finn drove away from the monastery.

AJ assumed they would go back to the villa and pick up the second rental car later, but was surprised when Finn passed the turn off and kept driving. Maire stared out the passenger window. She gripped her phone, her fingers flexing around it, itching to read Sebastian's journal, but Ethan kept glancing over his shoulder at her.

Throughout the drive, AJ kept her head down, occasionally peeking at Finn. He hadn't looked directly at her since he'd caught her at the stairs, but every so often his eyes met hers in the rearview mirror before flashing away. His shoulders were tight and that telltale tic flexed along his jaw. She turned to stare out her own window. She was in the doghouse. Had known she'd end up there as soon as Maire discovered Sebastian's journal in his library. Why hide the journal where only Maire could find it unless it had something to do with the stones?

The last thing Finn wanted to hear about were the stones. They had put that chapter of their lives behind them. The only person keeping it alive was Maire. Ethan had kept a stone should they want to go back to their time. Maire was only with them now because of her knowledge of the Book and the stones. She'd been kidnapped twice for that knowledge. A third time wasn't inconceivable if there were others who knew of the stones.

Finn wouldn't want them poking at fate. Yet, here they were. Secrets. Hidden in Sebastian's journals and between the women and the men. She could drive herself mad with what-ifs and had to stop second-guessing her decisions. Finn would have stopped them. Maire wouldn't have been satisfied. What if something else was brewing with the stones? Something that could impact them here and now? Finn had to understand that.

The knock at her window made her jump. Finn stood outside staring down at her. She glanced around, out of sorts. They were parked across the street from Guerin's. Everyone was already halfway across the street. She looked up at Finn. No smile, but he didn't look mad.

He opened the door and held out his hand. She took it and gave him a tentative smile.

"I should be angry with you." He closed the door and stepped forward, forcing AJ against the SUV.

It was difficult to look at him, so she stared at his chin. "I know."

"And I was. Every minute Ethan and I waited for the three of you to come up, my anger grew. Then you stepped up from those sketchy stairs, and I saw how confident you were. Your exhilaration from your little caper." He blew out a breath. "And I noted how defiant Maire looked as she glared at Ethan and me. I realized the position you were in. Stuck between your love for me and for Maire."

She dropped her forehead to his chest. "It was supposed to be harmless. Find Sebastian's library. It wasn't about the stones. Not in the beginning. Maire's been inconsolable not knowing what happened to Sebastian. I thought if there were more journals, it would satisfy her." She lifted her head and gazed into his warm emerald eyes. There was no judgment, only love. "I guess it got a bit out of control."

His grin made her heart thump wildly. Then he kissed her, and she melted into him, but he pushed her back too soon. "We need to get inside before Ethan's attacked by the women." She turned to go, but he gripped her arm. "You know my concern is for your safety, right?"

She took his hand, kissed it, then kept hold of it to lead him across the quiet street.

Guerin's was moderately busy with several open tables. Ethan had settled Stella and Maire at a corner table near the hearth but was currently at the bar.

"Don't they have waitstaff?" Finn asked as he glanced around.

AJ counted two waiters as they moved through the tables.

"I thought I'd wait here for you and AJ, but I did order a couple pitchers of cider."

She snorted. "Scared of being alone with the women?"

Ethan smiled. "Absolutely." He stood and held out an arm for AJ to go first.

When they arrived at the table, Stella glared at Ethan. "Decided it was safe to approach with bodyguards."

"Let it go, Stella." AJ dropped into a chair, suddenly bone weary. "Let's move past the whole who should have said what. We can work that out later. Besides, it's the holidays."

"You're right." Ethan's statement received raised eyebrows from Maire. "We have more important matters to discuss before we return to the villa. I think it would be best if Emory didn't hear this."

"I agree." Maire sat up and took a long sip of cider. She licked her lips, her gaze resting somewhere on the far side of the room before she turned back to us. "I'll start since I'm the one who can't let this rest. What I told you about Sebastian's journal was true—that he kept *The Book of Stones* split in its four parts, what each section would tell us, and that he decided to keep the stones and torc together. What I didn't mention was that he'd written another journal that he hid in the old smuggler's meeting room. He told me how to find it and that it was important for me to read." She took a bite of cheese and sipped more cider. Her forehead scrunched then she looked solemnly at each of them. "I'm sorry I made AJ and Stella keep this secret. But I had to get that other journal." She turned to Ethan and Finn. "I wasn't sure you'd let me find it, but I needed help." She sucked in a breath and gave a shaky smile, but her eyes were alive with an inner fire. "I haven't read more than the first couple of pages from this new journal, but Sebastian gave a quick overview. He discovered new incantations that provide more control of the time travel. He shared those details within the journal as well as the names of who received the four sections of the Book."

"I'm not sure I want to know." Ethan sat back, a bit glassy-eyed.

"Information isn't bad to have. It doesn't mean we have to act on it." Finn gripped his pint of cider, turning it slowly. "Since we have the journals, they should be fully translated so we know everything Sebastian thought important for us to know."

"And with any luck, we'll learn the location of the stones and torc. Right now, we're assuming they're still in the monastery." Stella worked on a swan, glancing up after finishing a fold.

"Maybe someone found them after Sebastian died." AJ didn't like the sound of it, but it had to be said.

"Let's hope he provides those details in this new journal," Ethan said.

The conversation turned to guesses of how the new incantations might work and who might have the sections of the Book. This turned into stories of their time in the past until Stella steered them to more optimistic talk about the holidays and what Helen was cooking for their evening meal.

"What have the two of you been up to with Adam these last few days?" AJ asked. When Finn and Ethan gave each other a side glance, she snorted.

"It appears we weren't the only ones with a secret." Maire folded her arms on the table, her questioning expression holding firm.

Stella placed a swan next to four others. "I don't think Finn was in the general store for barbecue implements." She lifted a brow. "And you've spent a lot of time at the marina." She paled. "This doesn't have anything to do with a boat does it."

Finn laughed. "I can guarantee there are no boats or water involved." He stretched his neck toward the door as someone exited. He nodded at Ethan. "Do you think it's time?"

Ethan placed money on the table. "I checked in. Adam said it's a go and that he needs the women back at the villa. Madelyn has already opened a second bottle of wine."

Stella stood at that announcement, forcing the others up. She didn't wait for them as she stormed toward the door. Everyone would think it was the mention of wine being opened that stirred Stella out the door. But that wasn't it. Stella was a sap when it came to the holidays. She didn't want anyone to know, and AJ had kept her secret, and she wouldn't even tell Finn that Stella's mad race to the door was for the surprise the men had waiting for them. It was Christmas Eve, after all.

AJ glanced down at the five swans sitting on the table and smiled at Stella's little gifts she left for the world.

17

On the way back to the villa, Finn stopped at the monastery so Ethan could collect the second rental car. Maire rode with him, leaving Stella with Finn and AJ. When they turned onto the street for the villa, Finn slowed their approach. Stella scooted up from the back seat until her head popped between Finn and AJ's, her focus pinned on the villa. When Finn came to a stop in the circular driveway, AJ and Stella opened their side windows for a better view.

The brisk evening air whipped through the car, and AJ held her jacket tight around her neck as she stared at the sight. Multi-colored Christmas lights had been strung across the front of the villa with white lights framing the doorway, the lights twisting around the front columns as they flowed to the ground. Two of the planters were also covered in tiny twinkling lights. Two spot-lights lit the tall firs, the colors rotating between blue, green, and red.

"You did this all today?" AJ whispered. When lights had started going up in Baywood, Finn had told her that Christmas wasn't a big event in his time, so he'd been amazed at how much effort people put into it now. His efforts to create this wonderful surprise touched her. She glanced over at Stella, who grinned from ear to ear.

"That was the plan, though Adam did the work with Helen and the kids when we left to look for you." He squeezed her shoulder. "And don't feel bad about that. I think he was pleased to have the kids help."

She touched his hand resting on her shoulder. "I'm sure he did. Mom would have loved it as well."

"Is there more?" Stella asked before she opened the car door and raced a few steps before stopping to take it all in again.

Ethan and Maire stepped next to Stella, his arm around Maire, whose head rested on his shoulder. Finn opened the door for AJ, and he took her hand. They stopped on the other side of Stella, and AJ grabbed her hand while she put an arm around Finn's waist. The five of them watched the lights for several long minutes before the front door opened. Adam, with his "Best Barbecue Dad" apron on, Madelyn, and Helen joined them and soon the children raced around the lawn.

Emory, who wore an apron with a floral design, hurried out. "I only have five minutes. I don't want the sauce to burn."

They all laughed as they stood as one to marvel at the lights as they twinkled with holiday charm. For now, at least where AJ was concerned, all thoughts of Sebastian, journals, and stones were pushed aside. This was time for family. She glanced at Maire, who was laughing at something Adam said, while Ethan seemed mesmerized by the lights. AJ nudged Finn, who looked over at his sister.

"This is the first time we've experienced Christmas like this." He gave AJ a squeeze. "It's been years since Maire and I celebrated it together."

"I'm glad I'm here to share it with both of you. And Ethan." AJ kissed him on the cheek. "Thank you."

He didn't say anything, and it was the first time since he'd been gravely injured in England, after being held prisoner by Reginald, that she could remember seeing tears fill his eyes. He'd thought he'd never see her again, but here they were, against all odds, and it made her heart sing with a joy she could barely contain.

"All right. Everyone back in the house. You can come out later with hot chocolate to stare at them, we have food waiting." Adam steered everyone back to the villa.

The front of the house wasn't the only change. Smells from the kitchen overwhelmed AJ, and her stomach immediately growled with anticipation. The scent of Mom's Christmas cookies overtook everything except for the fresh smell of fir. Garlands of holly and pine graced the entryway and flowed down the hall to the living room. Once again, the five people that just arrived stared at the Christmas tree that stretched fifteen feet high, barely missing the ceiling. Lights glittered off the ornaments, and strings of popcorn that started at the top circled the tree but stopped a few feet from the ground. A large bowl of popcorn with bits scattered over the floor sat next to two rolls of string and a pair of scissors, where the kids had been working before being interrupted by the group's arrival. Three empty glasses of milk and a crumb-covered plate had been abandoned on a nearby table. A bottle of wine and two partially filled glasses remained on the coffee table. AJ wiped at her eyes. It had been years since she'd felt like part of the family during the holidays, and she couldn't think of any other place she'd rather be.

Stella plopped down next to Charlotte, who pushed the bowl of popcorn toward her, then showed her how to string the popcorn. AJ left them laughing and joined her mother in the kitchen. She gave her a hug.

"This was the best thing we could have done." AJ wiped at her eyes again.

"We would have pulled something together at home, but you're right." Helen glanced around the kitchen and out toward the living room where most had gathered. "There's something special about being here in this place." Helen sipped a fresh glass of wine.

"If only Dad could be here."

Helen pushed a strand of hair from AJ's face and tucked it behind her ear. "But he is, honey. He always is."

"Helen, do you think this is done?" Emory called from the oven. He had the door open and was peering in.

Helen laughed. "I better go see. He could answer the question on his own, but he likes to hear my opinion."

AJ watched her mother bend down next to Emory, and his arm rested across her shoulders as they whispered. She wasn't sure where their romance was going, but she would support them anyway she could. They all needed a chance at love, even a second time. She thought of Stella. Stella didn't seem ready to settle down, but after seeing her with the family, maybe the tide was shifting. AJ wouldn't set her up, but it couldn't hurt to find opportunities that brought new people into their lives.

"AJ." Finn touched her shoulder. "Come get a glass of wine. Adam says we'll need our stamina for dinner and presents. Although I don't understand what that meant."

She turned and let him lead her to the living room where Stella was still on the floor with the kids. With the popcorn string completed, she'd returned to origami, this time folding paper in shades of pink, blue, and purple. Charlotte placed each completed shape on the Christmas tree while Patrick and Robbie tried their hand at creating an animal.

"I think Adam was referring to the lengthy process of children opening packages, and my mother's incessant need to take a photo each time they open something. We'll definitely want a comfortable spot."

"Perhaps we should prepare for the event with a lengthy bath. I believe you owe me one from this morning." He nibbled at her neck and goosebumps raced up her arms.

She pushed him away, unable to stop her giggles. "You will just have to wait until it's our private time to open presents."

"Hmm." He wrapped her in his arms and turned them toward the tree. "It will be difficult, but it sounds worth waiting for."

"Finn said you needed a few minutes by yourself. Are you okay?" Stella stood at the bedroom door until AJ waved her over.

AJ huddled in a stuffed chair by the window with her legs tucked under her. "I just needed time before the next round of merriment."

Stella laughed and took the chair next to her. "I had no idea your family could do so much in one day. It tired me out just thinking about it."

After a moment, AJ set down her cup of tea, her moment of solitude gone and probably for the best. She was growing melancholy again, unable to let go of the past that kept reinserting itself at the worst times. "The sea has always calmed me. Even on gray stormy days."

"And imagine you marrying a sea captain."

She snorted. "Destiny or fate?"

"What's the difference?"

They both chuckled.

Stella picked popcorn crumbs off her sweater. "I can't believe Ethan bought Maire an ice cream maker."

"You know how much Maire loves her ice cream."

"I guess enough to be making some as we speak."

AJ stared at Stella, her mouth open. "No way. She couldn't wait until we got home?"

Stella shook her head and stretched her legs out on the nearby coffee table. "Your mother claimed they just happened to have all the necessary ingredients."

"I smell a conspiracy."

"Oh, absolutely." Stella pulled at her hands, and AJ knew there was something on her mind. And with no paper in sight to make her shapes, she didn't seem to know what to do.

"Just say it."

Stella stared out the windows to a dark sea. "You're worried about Maire. That she might go back."

AJ released the breath she'd been holding since watching Maire open the ice cream maker. Maire had been smiling ever since leaving the monastery. She told herself Maire was just happy to have Sebastian's final words. But had he given her that? The only thing Maire mentioned was the Book. Granted, she hadn't had time to read the last journal and would probably be up half the night doing just that. In the end, it wouldn't matter what else Sebastian had to say, Maire's focus would be on that elusive book. Something Maire wanted to read from cover to cover since first learning about it.

"Stop thinking about it." Stella's tone was chiding, but AJ shook herself anyway.

She wiped her face with her hands. "You're right. Live for the day."

"Exactly. If she decides to go home, there's nothing you can do to stop that. No more than your desire to come home to the present. There's no right or wrong here. It's what calls to a person." Stella tapped the arm of the chair, the soft drumming nothing more than light thuds on the soft fabric. "Maire's smart and the most patient person I've ever met. She won't make a rash decision. There's still time."

AJ glanced toward the window. "I know all of that. I do." She ran her hands over her arms as if she was fighting off a shiver. "But there's a storm coming. I can feel it. I can't put my finger on anything specific, but the minute Maire found the hiding spot in the smuggler's meeting room, my gut clenched. I don't know what shape it will take, or who it will involve, but something is coming."

"Well, now I'm sorry I came to check on you."

AJ sat up, dropping her feet to the floor. "Wow, I have no idea where that came from."

Stella gave her an odd stare, then grinned. "I think this calls for a change in attitude and only one thing can do that."

"Oh." AJ forced a smile, though she was curious as to what Stella was cooking up.

"My root beer floats."

"Oh my, God. You haven't made those in years!"

"Can you imagine what they'll taste like with homemade ice cream?" Stella grabbed her hand and pulled her up.

"But you need root beer."

"We have root beer."

AJ snatched her hand back as she followed Stella into the hall. "Looks like my mother wasn't the only one with early knowledge of an ice cream maker." She attempted a sullen tone.

"Look at it this way. Maire has a new toy, and it's one she can't take back to her own time. With how much she loves ice cream, maybe it will give you time to convince her that this time is now hers."

That single statement was enough to lighten AJ's mood. At least for the rest of the evening.

Finn watched AJ and Stella emerge from the hall and it only took a single glance to know her smiling face was a facade for the group. The past had a life of its own, a habit of seeping into one's pores and twining its branches around your heart. He'd found a way to parse the good memories from the bad, but it hadn't happened overnight. AJ would find her peace, but even he had to admit, until Maire decided her path, nobody would find safe harbor from the stones. Discovering not one but two of Sebastian's journals could only spell trouble. But there was nothing for it except to get her mind off her worries for as long as he could. He met her as she approached the kitchen.

"I knew the ice cream would lure you out." Finn kissed her temple.

"You know me so well, do you?" AJ teased.

He leaned in. "I believe I mentioned long ago that I know you quite well. Shall I remind you of all the ways I know you?" He smiled when he saw her blush. He kissed the tip of her nose. "I think I've made my point." And he chuckled when she elbowed him and tugged at the end of her curls that were growing past her shoulders. He loved her short haircuts, but he let his fingers roam through the soft tendrils and considered changing his mind.

Finn turned to the kitchen where Maire was measuring ingredients. "My sister, who can't cook, seems to have found her passion with an ice cream maker. Who would have thought it?" Everyone laughed, and Maire stuck her tongue out, but there was a flicker of merriment in her gaze before she turned back, pouring milk while she swayed to the Christmas music.

He scanned the island with the myriad bowls of nuts, sauces, fresh fruit, and little bits of rainbow colors. "What are those?" He pointed to the rainbow dots.

"Sprinkles." Patrick stood a little taller and shook his head. "They're for kids."

"Oh. And what do you prefer on your ice cream?"

"Chocolate sauce, nuts, and..." He studied the bowls then looked at the other counter. "Hey, Dad, where are the marsh-mallows?"

"Ah, they're over here." Adam handed a bowl to Robbie. "Don't drop them."

"I won't." Robbie whined, but he had a smile on his face as he popped a tiny white morsel in his mouth.

"Marshmallows?" Finn wasn't sure that was an appropriate combination of items.

"Adam makes homemade rocky road ice cream," Helen explained. "It's typically made with chocolate ice cream, but the chocolate sauce will do when we only have vanilla." Helen held Charlotte in front of her as the little girl stared with big eyes at all the treats.

Finn shook his head, unfamiliar with the flavor.

AJ leaned in. "We'll drive up to Tillamook when we get home. There's a dairy where we can taste test ice cream. Maire will go nuts."

Finn would have to take her word for it. Adam hovered next to Maire, making suggestions and explaining terms that he pointed out in the recipe book. The man continued to fascinate him. When he'd first met Adam, he had a completely different impression of the hard-headed, if terrified, lawyer. He'd never pictured a family man who roasted his own coffee beans, made homemade ice cream, and had declared himself king of the barbecue. It was a wonder he had time to be a lawyer.

Once everyone had a bowl of ice cream or a mug of root beer float, they settled in front of the Christmas tree. The kids' presents were open, some back under the tree, others scattered across the floor. Maire's ice cream maker and a few other small presents were the only ones the adults opened. Any other gift giving would be shared privately or during lunch the following day. The weather was predicted to be gray and cold for their drive into the countryside, but Adam had found a pub a couple of hours away that would be open. He reserved a table and paid a deposit to ensure the owner would have food and drink ready.

He and AJ would share their presents later that evening, after they spent time with family.

"Are we driving with any destination in mind tomorrow? Maybe stopping every once and a while to take pictures?" Emory asked, licking the spoon from his float.

"There are a few small towns with quaint shops from what someone in town told me. They won't be open, but I hear they have great window displays." Madelyn seemed quite excited, but Adam rolled his eyes.

Finn leaned back in the sofa, AJ nestled beside him. He was a lucky man. The two of them had come so far in such a short amount of time. Dangerous times. And now they were at peace with opportunities on the horizon. Never before had he been so happy. Even his days sailing on the *Daphne* paled in comparison. His first ship would always have a warm spot in his heart. She'd kept him sane during his months of time travel, but not even she could compare to the love he felt for this woman beside him.

He glanced at Maire. Her smile was infectious, and he wished she'd do more of it. She'd grown pensive over the time she'd spent with Beckworth. Had that always been her fate or was she irrevocably changed by her long captivity? Her love for Ethan was apparent to him, if not to others. And now she had Sebastian's journals that could lead to reassembling *The Book of Stones*. He tightened his hold around AJ, knowing she must struggle with the same thoughts.

AJ looked up at him and touched his cheek. "I'm going to help Mom in the kitchen."

"I'll stay here until the hot cocoa is ready." He gave her his wicked lopsided grin, and his chest tightened when her eyes warmed with love.

When she strolled away, Ethan dropped into a chair next to him. "I'm not sure I can take anymore history lessons. They are actually speaking Celtic."

Finn glanced over to where his sister and Emory conversed. Patrick sat close, listening intently. Perhaps a future historian in the making. "I'm sure they weren't talking about you." Finn chuckled when Ethan preened.

"Of course not."

"So, when are you going to ask her to marry you?"

Ethan shot a quick glance in Maire's direction and then to where Adam, Stella, and Madelyn were watching Charlotte and Robbie add their origami figures to the tree. He lowered his voice. "Maire has spent most of the last three years in captivity. Now, she's been given a view into the future, where there are more freedoms here for women than Maire could ever achieve in our own time. Yet the past calls to her. If I didn't already know it before, the last few days of the women's plotting have confirmed it."

"Aye. She's caught between two worlds. AJ never questioned her desire to return to her own time, though I think she would have stayed if I couldn't follow, even if the rest of her heart would always be in this time. Since I'd been in the future, I knew I could be happy here as long as I had AJ."

"I feel the same way about your sister. As much as I'd missed this family I've been lucky enough to become a part of, I would gladly follow Maire home to the past. But until she makes a decision on which path is the right one, I don't want to be another worry she has to consider. She knows she has my support and my love. But marriage, if we were to return to the past, has to be considered carefully."

"Understandable. Who knew my sister had such patience to work through everything? But I suppose time taught her that as well." He studied Ethan, understanding the man's angst. "As they say in this time, give her space. I can't predict what she'll do, though I have a fairly decent thought on that. Patience on your part is a wise decision."

Ethan turned his gaze to Maire, and Finn grunted. An Englishman. What would their ma and da say about that? But he married an American. He chuckled and ignored Ethan's questioning glance.

"Listen up," Helen called from the kitchen doorway. "It's hot chocolate time. Come get a mug and let's go watch the lights."

AJ made up two mugs of cocoa, mini-marshmallows filling the top of hers. She handed Finn his mug sans marshmallows. They followed the group as everyone congregated in the foyer, helping to hold mugs while others put on their coats. She took Finn's hand when the group moved to the front drive where someone, probably Adam, had set up folding chairs.

Instead of sitting, she snuggled into Finn's broad chest and turned to watch the twinkling lights. The group was quiet as they drank and whispered. Without warning, Emory began singing "Deck the Halls" and soon everyone joined in with the exception of Finn, Ethan, and Maire, who knew the melody but not the words. Then Maire sang an Irish melody that only Finn and Emory knew, their strong voices a beautiful contrast to Maire's. Stella couldn't leave well enough alone and belted out an excellent rendition of "Rockin' around the Christmas Tree" that got everyone smiling and swaying. Cheers erupted when Emory swung Helen around the driveway as they danced and sang along. Then Madelyn dragged Adam out to show everyone they knew a few steps of their own. For the finale, Emory started them off with "O Come, All Ye Faithful" which everyone knew.

Afterward, the group quieted again. AJ felt Stella's gaze on her, but she didn't turn that way. Stella was worried about her and there wasn't anything she could say to change that. So, she pulled Finn down to give him a long, slow kiss. If that didn't convince Stella everything was all right, nothing would.

Adam stepped out in front of everyone and turned his back on the twinkling display. He held up his mug. "I know it's not New Years, but I think this needs to be said. This time last year, there were seven of us. Now there are twelve. We are a truly blessed family, and whatever the future holds, we'll always stay family."

"Here, here," Finn yelled and put his other arm around Stella, who had gravitated closer.

Now, AJ took the time to turn to her friend and smile. "Here, here."

18

Waverly Estate - England - 1804

Beckworth entered the kitchen the morning after Christmas to find Eleanor, his dear friend from London, who now lived a short distance away, banging pots and pans as she washed them. Something from the oven smelled delicious, and fresh bread loaves sat on a counter.

"What's all this?" Beckworth looked around for a coffee cup, grabbed a tin mug instead, and poured coffee from the kettle by the hearth. He took a gratifying sip then shuffled to a chair at the servant's table.

"Someone needs to feed your guests a hearty breakfast before they leave." Eleanor pulled out a pan from the oven.

"The kitchen staff already left food for us. I thought—who was it Mrs. Walker told me?—Doris, I think. She was supposed to help until the guests left."

"I sent her back home and told her to take tomorrow off as well."

Beckworth lifted a brow but couldn't help a smile. "You don't have to mother me."

"I'm simply giving your hard-working servants some time off."

"You mean my well-paid servants."

She gave him a wink over her shoulder. "Doesn't matter. People still need time off with their families. Besides, I haven't seen Ellingsworth for months. And she wanted an early start this morning. I hear Mary—is that her name?—Hensley's wife, is eager for the trip. I'm becoming as feeble as you at remembering things."

"Yes. It happens with fine living. So, I suppose this means the table has already been set?"

"Of course. I did that while the bread was baking."

He shook his head. "What can I do?"

"I set the service in your office. I thought you and the men could take breakfast there. You just need to be the viscount for another few hours. Then I thought we'd spend the day together."

"Marvelous." He stepped next to her and placed a kiss on her temple before jumping back as she whacked him with a large spoon. He barely kept his coffee from sloshing out of the mug, but he laughed. "You're still faster than me."

"Always will be," she called out as he made his way toward his office.

He drank his coffee while moving chairs around so his visitors would be comfortable. He enjoyed the day after Christmas when most of the servants had the day off. There were times when he just wanted to be Beckworth and not a viscount. He enjoyed what wealth had brought him, but now that the duke and Dugan wasn't dictating his every move, he found the life as a viscount somewhat dull.

His estate manager ran everything and did it well. After all the time Beckworth had been absent from his estate, he thought he'd come home to find it deep in debt. But it was just the opposite, no doubt with some help from Barrington. It was as if he'd only been gone a fortnight. He'd hoped to become more involved with Corsham, the nearby town, and its townspeople. Some of the business owners had gotten to know him and accepted him, yet others were still leery of his motives from his earlier days as the viscount. He couldn't blame them.

Now, he smelled something afoot. But from what direction? His first scent came from whatever games Lady Prescott and Gaines had been playing. However, the recent news Hensley had received about this mystery spy called Gemini intrigued him. He tugged at his sleeves as he studied his office, pleased with everything in its place. One thing was certain, he didn't think he'd be bored for long.

A knock came at the door before Jamie pushed it open with his boot. He carried a tray filled with heavenly aromas.

"Don't tell me I have to pay you a footman's wage." Beckworth pointed to a side table.

"I know better than to expect anything so grand from you." Jamie laughed and turned as Fitz followed him in with the coffee service.

Beckworth glanced at the food and then at the door. "Where's Hensley? I expected him to follow in with the rest of the food."

"He's saying his farewells to Mary and Dame Ellingsworth. Eleanor said the rest of the food is on its way."

Fitz poured coffee for himself and Jamie, then topped off Beckworth's cup. "I'm looking forward to a hearty meal, some devious planning, then a nice ride back to the ship." He settled onto the sofa with a baleful look at the sideboard.

"Did you enjoy the hunt yesterday?" Beckworth opened serving trays to see what Eleanor had put together. Looked like

Fitz would get his wish on a good meal. "I don't think I saw you after that."

"The hounds took us on a merry tour of the countryside. By the time we got back, there were people everywhere. Thought it best to get out of the way." Fitz craned his neck to look out the doorway. "Will Hensley be coming soon?"

Jamie hit Fitz on the back of this head. "You can wait a few more minutes. And you were doing so well at playing gentleman this weekend."

Fitz scowled then jumped up, almost tripping over his feet in his haste to help Eleanor with another tray of food.

Eleanor gave him a tolerant smile. "Hensley's on his way. He just walked the women to their carriage." She glanced at Fitz and gave him a nod, holding out an empty plate. "Might as well have someone taste this casserole. I can make something else if it didn't turn out right."

Fitz settled back on the sofa with a plate of eggs and meat. He scooped a heaping fork into his mouth, and his eyes closed as he chewed. After a large swallow, he opened his eyes, and Beckworth could have sworn the man was teary-eyed.

"I'll take that as positive sign." Eleanor turned to Beckworth. "If you need anything else, I'll be collecting the linen."

"You don't have to do that." Beckworth tried not to growl. He hated when Eleanor worked like a housemaid.

"No. I don't. But it's one less thing for the staff to care for tomorrow. I'll let them do the washing. At least the rooms will be clean. Now get to your meeting or your guests won't see Bristol until well after dark."

Hensley met Eleanor at the door, and he stepped aside to let her pass. He smiled. "That is one amazing woman."

"She can be worse than a mother hen." Beckworth waited for Jamie and Hensley to collect their breakfast before fixing a plate.

"And you'd be lost without her." Hensley sat in the chair next to Beckworth's desk and tasted the eggs. After everyone agreed the meal was more than worthy, he got down to business. "As you know, I received word from one of my men in London. They believe Gemini is on the move." Hensley wiped his mouth and leaned back, his stomach making an ample table for his plate. "They believe he's heading west toward Bristol."

"I thought you didn't know who Gemini was?" Jamie finished his plate and handed it to Fitz, who took the opportunity to fill a plate for himself as well as the captain.

"We don't. Not for sure. There are two men we've been tracking, who are rumored to work for Gemini. This group, we're not sure what else to call it at this point, keeps a very loose structure. They never meet in large groups and disseminate information from man to man. I've had scouts follow them, but their activities appear scattered. Without additional information as to the identity or possible whereabouts of this Gemini, I have no recourse but stay the course. Bringing them in for questioning would do little good if we weren't able to break them, and then all we would have done is shown our hand, what little we have, to Gemini. These two men have never traveled together or in the same direction, until now. We're hoping this is a break. Perhaps when Gemini becomes active, the men begin to gather." He stopped and took a moment to wipe his brow before taking a long drink of coffee. "I know the information is weak, but there you have it."

"Maybe they were coming to Waverly for a nice holiday gathering." Jamie gave Beckworth a smile. "Maybe Lord Melville himself."

"Or perhaps that Barkley fellow, although he seemed rather stuffy. He lives just west of here, doesn't he?" Hensley wasn't serious, but Beckworth had to chuckle.

"Lord Nash. While that would be an interesting twist, he's not very smart. Although, I hear his family money is running out. People do strange things when facing debt collectors." Beckworth considered his guests, but no one fit the bill. Except for one—Gaines. But who would the second man be if they appeared to be traveling together?

"Maybe Lord..." Fitz scratched his head and then his chest. "I can't remember their names. He's the one married to Lady Agatha."

"Lord Osborne?" Beckworth shook his head with a snort. "He's not bad at strategy, if you rely on his ability to play a good game of chess. But he's not someone who enjoys intrigue other than hearing about another's adventures. He's quite settled in his ways."

"Remember what Maire told us." Jamie's tone turned serious. "Gemini could be a woman."

They all stopped to consider that, then they grinned.

"Wouldn't that be something." Hensley finished his plate and set it on the desk before giving his waistcoat a good wiping of crumbs.

"So maybe Lady Agatha herself," Jamie said. "She seemed devious enough to set up a spy ring."

"I don't see it." Fitz settled back in his seat, satisfied after three helpings of breakfast. "She's good at handing out directions, but she's rather single minded and prefers to manipulate those around her for petty satisfaction."

"Fitz. I told you to leave the married women alone." Jamie shook his head, and Hensley blushed.

Fitz shrugged. "I would also cross Lady Melville off your list. That one's a talker. She knows everyone's secrets. You'd have known straight away if she was Gemini."

"Maybe that raven-haired woman who has all the available men pursuing her." Jamie studied the ceiling. "Lady Prescott."

That suggestion registered with Beckworth with the woman's

unexpected appearance and secret meetings with Gaines. But an infamous spy? Had she been the one whispering in Reginald's ear, or maybe Dugan's? Anything was possible at this point.

"I don't know." Fitz leaned back, a leg across his knee. "For all her seductiveness, she expected me to do all the work."

Jamie laughed, and this time Hensley just shook his head.

Beckworth stared at Fitz, recalling the day of the first hunt. Fitz had entered the solarium just after Lady Prescott exited with a group taking a tour of the garden. He could still remember the flush on her cheeks. Then he remembered Libby's comment about Lady Agatha and Fitz. "Have you slept with all my guests?" His voice came out in a high-pitched whine that made him shudder. He wasn't sure if he was upset, impressed, or jealous. *Bloody hell.*

Fitz considered the question before shaking his head. "Only the women." When Hensley coughed, Fitz turned a deep red then held his hands out in defense. "Not Mary, my Lord. I would never think it."

"I would think not." Hensley's voice was stern, but his gaze twinkled. "I think she'd rather fill you with crumpets."

"Aye." Fitz got that dreamy look in his eyes whenever food was mentioned.

"What did you think of that Gaines fellow?" Beckworth asked the room at large, fishing for other opinions while attempting to erase the images of Fitz with his female guests.

"He didn't speak much." Jamie filled coffee cups. "Although I did see him speaking with Lady Prescott a time or two."

"Did they know each other?" Beckworth doubted Jamie knew but was interested in his impression.

Jamie, as usual, gave it full consideration before shaking his head. "No. At first I thought he might be flirting, but I don't remember her smiling. Come to think of it, she only smiled after she walked away from him. There was a stark difference in her beauty when she smiled."

"I only met Gaines once, but I agree with Jamie. The man didn't speak, seemed to just hover on the edges. Who did he arrive with?" Hensley asked.

"Came with the Melvilles." Fitz returned to the buffet service and selected two sweet breads.

"No. Melville told me Gaines met them on the drive in." That had been the moment Beckworth became interested. But a spy? Then what was he doing with Lady Prescott?

"A mystery to be sure." Hensley shifted in his seat, and with nothing more to discuss on Gemini, switched to his favorite subject. "So, Jamie, what did you think of that new stallion I bought?"

They spoke of trivial things for another hour before Jamie stood and smacked Fitz on the shoulder.

"It's time to get back to the ship. We leave for Dublin in the morning."

Fitz stood, brushed crumbs off his pants, then stretched. "A good ride before a sail is a blessing."

They filed out of the office and through the east entrance to where Hensley's carriage waited for him. Jamie and Fitz mounted their horses and waited for Hensley since they would share the same road for most of the journey.

Before getting into the carriage, Hensley took Beckworth aside. "I only mentioned Gemini so you could keep an ear open. Don't investigate it."

Beckworth studied the man. "You don't want to catch him."

Hensley smiled. "Not yet. I want to see who he's working with. It has to be someone with influence."

Beckworth nodded. He didn't have time to worry about Gemini. He had business in London, including the tailor

Hensley wanted him to visit. And who knew if Lady Prescott would cross his path again?

"I'm serious, Beckworth." Hensley frowned. "You're a resource I want to keep around."

Beckworth chuckled. "I always knew you cared. But I don't follow as easily as Murphy."

A shadow passed over Hensley's face for the briefest moment before it was replaced with a gentle smile. "I hope he and AJ found peace."

Beckworth felt a tug in his chest that bothered him more than he expected. "If it's one thing I learned, Murphy always landed on his feet, and AJ is too stubborn to give up her dreams."

"You've hit the mark, my friend." Hensley turned to the carriage and climbed in. He leaned his head out the window. "Do as I say, Beckworth. It's the most sensible thing you could do."

Hensley waved his hand, and the carriage began to roll. As Hensley passed by, Beckworth gave him a wink. Sensible had never quite fit.

19

Northern France - Present Day

AJ leaned against Finn, one leg kicked out from beneath the sheet. She ran a finger over the silver pendant—a replica of the *Daphne Marie*. The silver work so intricate, she could make out small gunports and a crow's nest on top of a mast with unfurled sails. It hung from a silver rope chain that looked similar to the lines used onboard a ship.

"It's beautiful." Tears threatened, but she pushed them back. "They'll always be with us, won't they?"

Finn pulled her close, his cheek resting on her head. "Aye, always."

She laughed. "I would never have thought a ship could mean so much. Or bring back so many wonderful memories."

"The ones where we're running for our lives or battling storms?"

"All of it. And maybe those were the times that meant the most. Surviving against all odds."

He took the necklace from her hand and placed it around her neck, fastening the lock. He kissed her temple. "I was going to give this to you sooner, but the jeweler was a fussy man."

"And I'm glad he was. It's perfect. I'd love to see the sketch you gave him."

She pulled away from him. "Now, your turn." She crawled across the bed on her hands and knees to the hat-sized red and green box. "Are you staring at my backside?" She turned with the box held in both hands and grinned when she noticed where his gaze had settled.

He returned her grin with a rakish one of his own. "I'm staring at two lovely presents. Whatever you have in that box and my beautiful wife."

"Flattery might just get you more than you expected."

His brows rose as his grin grew wider. When he reached for her, she pulled back, pushing the box toward him.

"Oh, no. Open your present first." She winked. "You'll be glad you did." Then she sat back on her heels. "At least, I think you will."

He took the box. "Well, let's see what has turned Mrs. Murphy into such knots."

AJ's heart pounded. It was stupid. It was just a gift. But somehow it represented their crazy beginning. The question was whether it would mean as much to him as it did to her. She was the antique lover, and this was nothing more than an everyday instrument. He took great care with the box, slowly opening each tab, and her heart squeezed at his childlike joy of the gift. His locks fell over his forehead, his eyes narrowed as he investigated what was under all the multiple sheets of tissue paper.

Then he stopped. And stared. AJ's heart rate increased, her nerves buzzing between excitement and doubt. A full minute went by before he pulled the gift out. A sextant. It wasn't an exact match to the one on the *Daphne*, but it was close to the same time period, and she doubted they differed much.

He glanced up. His eyes were shiny, and the love reflected in them took her breath away.

"I visited the antique store on Main Street. It was the same day we ran into you at the general store. I mean, I'm an antiques broker. Of course, I'm going to check it out." She was babbling and couldn't stop. Finn's grin filled his face, just as handsome as the first day she'd seen him on the dock at the inn. Maybe more so, knowing how much he'd done for her.

She took a deep breath and continued more slowly. "I saw it on my first pass through the store but wasn't sure. Then I couldn't get it out of my head so I thought—why not?"

"Because it speaks to you as much as it does to me."

Her cheeks heated. After all this time and everything they'd been through, he could still make her blush. She took the sextant from him and held it as he'd taught her. "I'm not sure I remember all the steps."

"And what star should we use tonight? Arcturus again?"

"The North star."

His brow went up. "Really?"

She ran a hand down his cheek. "Because you're my true north. And as long as you're with me, I'll never get lost."

"Now who's the romantic, Mrs. Murphy." He took the sextant from her hands and dropped it on the floor. "I request one more present."

She began to back up, a giggle trying to worm its way out. "And what might that be?"

"I'd like to see you with nothing on but that necklace."

Two hours later, AJ sprawled across Finn, her breathing finally slowing after another round of love making. She was going to like holidays. The thought made her smile, and she turned her head to find Finn staring at her with a lopsided grin. "No. I can barely move."

He chuckled. "Get your mind out of the gutter, Mrs. Murphy."

She harrumphed and crawled up to lie next to him, her head resting comfortably in the crook of his arm. She rolled into him and swung a leg over his. "I'll never get tired of this."

"Well, that's promising."

She gave him a playful slap. "I can't remember the last time we laid in bed, so pleased with the world."

"We'll always find time to hide away in our own world."

"Where no one can touch us."

He grasped her hand. "I know you've been hurting, wondering what Maire will do."

She didn't want to talk about it. Not now.

He squeezed her hand. "My sister and I were so close when we were young. We could finish each other's sentences and somehow always knew where the other one was. But after our parents died, I felt a different responsibility to her. We were still close, but it wasn't the same. I became hard. Then before I knew it, I had my own ship and spent far too much time at sea. It's only now, in this time period, that the two of us have begun to remove the distance between us." He shifted, turning toward her to play with the necklace he'd given her. "It will break my heart if she goes back, but it's not my life. She must live her own journey. Wherever, or whenever, that happens to be."

"I know. But I never realized how well we'd get along. How much I'd love her." She buried her head in Finn's chest and sighed. "Okay. I got it out. I think I'll be better now."

"Maire is a patient woman. And until she figures out a way for that ice cream maker to work in the past, I don't think she'll be going anywhere."

"There does seem to be some truth in that." Stella had told

her as much. Maire liked ice cream more than a person should. Would there soon be little cartons in the grocery aisle with Maire's smiling face on them? She snorted at the thought. The woman had enough determination.

"I have an idea." He leaned into her, his kiss full of promise. "Let's make a baby."

"I thought we agreed to wait until the remodeling was done."

"Aye. But nothing says we can't practice. Merry Christmas, my sweet lass."

Concern for Maire slipped away. Her friends were right. Live in the present and enjoy each memory she makes with her amazing family. The world would always be there. And if something was coming, they'd face it together like they always did. A peace settled over her as she lay in Finn's embrace, ready for whatever their future held.

BOOK 7 PREVIEW - A STONE DENIED

Thank You For Reading!

I hope you enjoyed spending time with AJ, Finn, and all their family and friends for holiday cheer...along with a bit of sleuthing.

I thought this series would end here, but two characters refused to be silenced. And rightly so. And well...the story of the stones isn't quite complete.

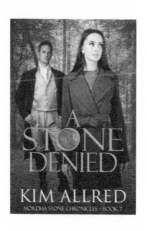

Available Now

Here's the first chapter of A Stone Denied

The stones and torc were hidden deep within the monastery. The four sections of The Book of Stones spread far and wide. The Heart Stone separated by two hundred years. They were supposed to be safe...

A Stone Denied
Mórdha Stone Chronicles, Book 7

Baywood, Oregon - Present Day

Stella Caldway grumbled as she stuffed the oversized mug of coffee into the cup holder. The lid came off and splashes of cream-colored liquid sprayed the console, passenger seat, and her long, cherry-red rain duster. "Damn." She opened the middle console and pulled out wadded up napkins, quickly soaking up the mess.

This was the second time of an already long morning she'd spilled coffee. The first time, right after she'd finished dressing, the coffee had run down her linen pants. After exchanging them for another pair, this time something a few shades darker, she tried wiping the stain out but gave up and tossed the slacks into the dry-clean pile.

The coffee had also managed to spread to a client folder and seeped into the top pages of the final contract, where earlier, she'd fought with a recalcitrant printer. Sighing, she'd spent another thirty minutes reprinting the contract and creating a new folder.

Once the car's interior was clean and back to normal, Stella pushed her auburn hair back, checked her makeup in the visor mirror, glanced at her watch, swore to herself, then slid the car into drive to pull out of her small circular driveway.

She hated being late, priding herself on being the consummate professional. One thing she'd learned early on, very little in real estate ran on time. Inspectors ran late, customers wanted to see just one more house, sellers changed times when a house could be shown. It never bothered her. She found she could adapt to any situation, always diverting disgruntled homeowners or buyers with other distractions. The one thing she could control was herself.

However, this morning, she'd definitely woken on the wrong side of the bed. If she knew what was good for her, she'd cancel her meetings and go back to bed, but there were only two appointments, both for contracts with new customers. Her first meeting went without a hitch. One contract was signed with a commitment to have a list of houses for their review in two days. Their wish list was pretty simple for new homeowners, and based on the decor of their rental house, she'd already made a mental list of a couple homes they'd adore.

She stopped at a local coffeehouse for a refill, and with plenty of time before her next meeting, decided to head to the inn. Ever since the large group of family and friends had returned from their holidays in France three months ago, Finn had split his time between assisting Jackson with the remodeling of the inn and preparing his sailboat for a week-long trip down the coast of California.

AJ was excited for a little time away, but if Stella had to guess, her friend was more thrilled to see Finn's eagerness to set sail. She figured this was just the start of long sailing trips, and she'd be jealous if the thought of being on the waves didn't make her stomach do flips. Standing on a dock was enough to get her seasick.

Although AJ and Finn were probably hoping for time alone, everyone sighed with relief when Maire had suggested she and Ethan tag along. She'd locked herself away after France, eager to study the pages of Sebastian's two journals they'd discovered hidden in the monastery. After two months, Maire hadn't fully completed the translation. It turned out, of the two journals they'd found while on holiday at the monastery, Sebastian had used the second one to copy what he felt were the more prominent parts of *The Book of Stones* before he sent the four sections away to be protected. Maire determined there were missing pieces Sebastian hadn't copied but hoped that with more time, she might be able to make an educated guess on those gaps. That decision seemed to be enough for her to return to a normal routine, and everyone settled into their life.

Since Stella wouldn't be sailing with them, she agreed to watch the inn, stopping by every day to refill bird feeders and water the indoor plants. Jackson had taken the week off, and the sun had decided to show itself on what was turning out to be a lovely, early spring day.

She was turning into the inn's driveway when her phone rang. Checking the screen, she smiled and activated the speaker in the car. "Hi, Isaiah. What are you up to?"

Isaiah was Jackson's grandson, who had returned the previous summer from his travels to help with the inn's remodel. He was supposed to go back to California for the fall semester at a popular university but decided to finish his classes at the university in Eugene. Professor Emory had helped him transfer his transcripts and credits, having once been a tenured professor at the institution before retiring to buy an old bookstore.

"I'm on my way back to Baywood. I'm still an hour out but just got a ping from the inn's alarm."

"Really?" Stella slowed as she drove down the driveway. "I'm just now pulling in and don't see any other cars except the ones that belong here." She laughed. "It's probably that crazy seagull that AJ keeps feeding. I'm running late this morning, so I haven't put his snack out yet."

Isaiah chuckled, and he raised his voice to compete with the wind gusting in the background. "It's possible. It was definitely him two days ago."

"Yeah, the poop in front of the French doors was a dead give-away," Stella spoke louder and shivered, not understanding how he could drive over a mountain pass on a cool morning with the windows down.

"Ari seems to know how to make an entrance."

Ari, or Aristotle as AJ named him, was a one-eyed seagull that looked as if he had been in one too many bar fights. He'd somehow discovered AJ's soft spot for gulls and found his way to her back deck. Once she fed him, he became the inn's very own seagull, showing up every day at the same time, waiting for his snack. Turned out he was quite patient, and though he'd fluff his feathers in a disgruntled way, he always waited, no matter how long it took for someone to come home. Ethan was the one who started calling him Ari. He thought it was funny since Ari was a bird. No matter how hard AJ had tried to stop it, everyone now called him Ari except for her.

Stella parked her car and rolled down a window before shutting off the engine. She waited a beat. "I don't hear anything."

"Not even squawking?"

She shook her head then remembered to vocalize it. "No. But that's not unusual. He likes to surprise people."

Isaiah snorted. "And I just thought it was Grand Pops who did that."

Stella grinned. "Well then, I guess Ari is in good company." She got out of the car. "I think everything is okay."

"Maybe you should wait until I get there. Do you have time to come back later? Ari will wait, and so will the plants."

"I have a meeting in an hour, then just want to go home, soak in a hot bath, and forget this day happened."

"That bad?"

"You don't know the half of it."

"I'd still like you to wait. Or better yet, I'll feed Ari and cover your other tasks. I'd feel better."

"Tell you what. Since I'm already here, why don't I just slip in, see what mess Ari made this time, then call you back? Five minutes tops."

There was a long pause. "I'm not going to change your mind, am I?"

Stella mounted the stairs, pinched the phone between her ear and shoulder, then dug in her purse. "It's all quiet. If anyone was here, they would have heard me pull up then scrambled to get out. And with no car, how much could they steal? Probably early spring breakers, and worst case, Finn's stash of homebrew will be gone."

"Now that would be disastrous."

Stella laughed. "Five minutes, and I'll call you back." She hung up after she heard his grunt and tossed the phone in her purse while holding on to the set of keys she'd recovered. She opened the front door and breathed in the deep scent of cedar and lavender that always permeated the house. When she saw the mail on the side table, she cursed under her breath. She'd forgotten to grab the mail, considered walking up to retrieve it, then decided there was always tomorrow. Her purse dropped next to the stack of catalogs, bills, and other junk advertisements.

It was such a beautiful day, and her chores wouldn't take long. She would have time for a cup of coffee on the back deck. Might as well squeeze whatever enjoyment she could out of the day. AJ kept a variety of single-serve coffees, and she strode to the kitchen to start a cup brewing while she inventoried Ari's mess.

When she walked into the kitchen, she felt the chill and immediately found the broken window in the French doors. She raced over, hoping Ari hadn't flown through it and died. What would she tell AJ? It wasn't like running down to the local pet shop to buy a replacement goldfish.

She pulled to a stop and stared at the floor. Nothing but

broken glass.

"Ah, there you are."

She spun around, her hand sliding to her throat when her gaze fell on the tall stranger. Before she could turn to run, the man leaped toward her, and in two strides, grabbed her upper arm. Having taken some self-defense classes offered by one of the larger Realtor offices in town, she knew a thing or two. She turned into him and stomped on his foot with the stiletto heel of her boots.

The man screamed and released her, pulling his foot up like an injured paw. Stella shoved him and ran. He caught the edge of her rain duster, but she didn't stop, and the sound of the material ripping at its seams made her growl.

The only question was where to run. Finn still hadn't completed the panic room. AJ had drummed it into Stella that the library and the master bathroom were the safest places in the house. She headed for the library but switched mid-stride as she reached the staircase. The safety of the library was actually within the armory. They'd activated the alarm before leaving, and for some reason, her perfect memory was failing to come up with the code for the door. She didn't think she'd have time to figure it out. The scuff of boots scrambling on the slick hardwood floor ramped up her frenzy.

She took the stairs two at a time and had just reached the top when a hand grabbed her shoulder. Then she was tackled, falling hard on the landing with the man on top of her. She rolled, kicking and punching, a couple of her strikes connecting, but all the man did was grunt.

Then a piercing pain slammed into her head just before her vision winked out.

The tingling sensation became painful enough to wake Stella. When she moved her leg, she released a whimper. Not sure what had happened, she pried her eyes open, but the light was too bright. Her head pounded, and when she reached for it, discovered she couldn't move her hands. That forced her to take a peek through squinting eyes. She was back in the kitchen, tied to a dining room chair. Tied so tight, she was losing feeling in her hands and toes. That explained the pins and needles sensation.

The pounding in her head made it difficult to keep her eyes open, but she pulled herself together when the man entered the kitchen. She studied him more closely now that she wasn't running from him. He was dressed strangely, the tailoring all wrong. His worn jacket hung halfway to his thigh, and the collar of his shirt rose too high on his neck. His vest...she gulped... wasn't a vest but a waistcoat. Her chest tightened, threatening to close off her breath when a nagging truth slammed into her. This wasn't a thief. Well, he might be, but he'd come a long way to rob someone. Like maybe two-hundred-years long.

No. No. No.

Why hadn't she waited for Isaiah? Because she had been in a hurry. Because she didn't think anything truly bad could happen in Baywood. She stifled a self-deprecating laugh. Because she thought, as AJ and Finn had, that the nightmare with the stones was over. And she would bet every last cent of her very fat savings that this man was here because of the stones.

He leaned his hip against the counter, arms crossed over his chest, and his expression a bit wild-eyed, which didn't lend a comforting feeling.

"Where's the stone, Miss Moore?"

Stella blinked then shook her head, which only made the headache worse. "What?"

"The Heart Stone. It must be here for the smaller stone to have found you."

Yep. He was a thief. And if the clothing hadn't told her enough, his English accent confirmed it. She hated when she was right. And, of course, he had a stone, or he wouldn't be standing in AJ's kitchen. How long had she been unconscious? She glanced at the microwave. If she was reading the numbers correctly, only five minutes had passed. It seemed longer.

He gave the outward opinion of being calm—for the most part. He continued to lean back, his posture relaxed, but his gaze bounced about the room as if taking everything in but confused by what he saw. Her best guess was that this wasn't his first time jump to the future but hadn't jumped much more than that. A mixture of an extremely dangerous man and a scared rabbit. She was fairly certain that wasn't a safe combination.

"Who are you?" Her mouth was dry, and she glanced longingly toward the jug of water she used to water the plants.

"My name doesn't matter. What matters is what I came for. The Heart Stone. If you just give it to me, I can be on my way, and you can get back to..." he scowled as he waved at the kitchen in general "...however you live with all this."

"I don't know what you're talking about." Her head began to clear, and she bent her neck slowly from side to side, hearing a slight snap as pressure released and the ache receded, though it hadn't left entirely. Now that she could think, she retraced her steps since arriving. Then his earlier words came to her. He thought she was AJ. That made sense since she'd bounced through the door and into the kitchen like she owned the place.

He stared at the ceiling, seeming to contemplate his next move. He prowled around the dining room and kitchen, which were designed to be one spacious open space. Every time he passed to pace behind her, she went rigid as she waited. For what, she wasn't sure what to expect.

After the third pass, he grabbed her hair, pulling back so hard and fast that one moment she'd been staring at the horrifyingly slow movement of the clock on the microwave, and the next, she gazed at the ceiling. His grip was so tight, she was positive he'd rip her hair from her head as tears streaked down her face. The pounding in her head returned, but she refused to scream. Instead, she slammed her lids shut so she wouldn't have to look at his menacing face as he leaned over her.

His body odor and wickedly sour breath made her want to choke. "From everything I've heard about you, I figured you'd choose the hard way. So be it." While still clutching her hair, he raised a fist.

Before he could release the punch, she yelled, "Finn has it. All he told me was that he put it in a safe place. That I didn't have to worry about it anymore." The words raced out of her as she spun her tale. While she hated lying, she was pretty good at it. The fact she was terrified for her life added a huge dose of reality to her story.

The man paused, then slowly released her hair. Stella rolled her neck, and though she didn't feel the satisfying snap, the intense thrumming lessened. She blinked back tears and noticed the clock change. Isaiah was still forty minutes away.

When her view was blocked by a hulking form, she stared up to eyes full of doubt—or maybe confusion. He stood within striking distance though his arms were crossed again. "I don't believe you."

Without missing a beat and needing to stall for time, she went with a partial truth from something AJ had shared with her. "When we returned from the monastery, I wasn't myself." She glanced down and nibbled her lips. She lowered her voice. "I began seeing things—people who should have been long dead. I couldn't sleep, worried that a day like this might come." She sniffled for effect, then choked out a half-laugh. "Guess someone owes me a big apology."

After a silent moment, she lifted her chin and stared him in the eye, releasing part of her rage. "He decided it was best if I didn't know where he put the Heart Stone." She smirked. "He bought into that whole out of sight, out of mind theory."

He pulled away from the counter and stalked toward her.

She couldn't stop from daring to go a little farther. "It appears I was right all along. I'm hoping I'll live long enough to tell Finn I told you so." Did she want to know whether he was planning on killing her?

He smiled, though it wasn't very pleasant. "Now we have some honesty." He strode to the bay window and stared out to the shimmering ocean. Good fortune turned her way when he stood there for ten minutes before sighing. "I didn't want to do it this way, but we knew we might not have another option."

Stella wanted to scream. No one would hear her, but it might release the terror worming its way through her and picking up speed like an express train as he turned. She released an audible sigh when he walked past her.

He reached into his inside jacket pocket and pulled out two pages of parchment. He selected one and placed it in the center of the kitchen island, using the empty flower vase as a paperweight. The vase AJ always kept filled with fresh flowers from either her garden or Stella's. It sat empty while they were gone —two days away from being of any help to her

When he turned toward her, he pulled a knife from his boot. Her stomach dropped as if she'd plummeted from a penthouse window. She shook uncontrollably and couldn't stop, even when all he did was cut the bindings to her arms and legs.

She immediately moved her hands and feet around, rubbing each wrist and grimacing as the blood rushed into her extremities. He turned his back on her for a moment as he pulled out another smaller piece of parchment. Stella didn't wait to see what it was.

She was up, flying through the kitchen and rounding the corner, making one more attempt at the stairs and the master bathroom. She didn't even make the stairs before a fist grabbed her hair and pulled her to a stop.

"You are a foolish woman," he hissed and spun her around.

She kicked him in the shin and swore. She'd been aiming a lot higher. Before she could regroup, he slapped her so hard, she understood the phrase "seeing stars." At the same time, he kicked her legs out from under her, then grabbed an arm along with her hair and dragged her back through the kitchen toward the French doors. He stopped long enough to open the door. Her raincoat protected her from the broken glass scattered on the floor. She continued to protest as he lifted her by the waist and pulled her through the door.

Once they were on the back deck, he fished in his pocket and retrieved a small piece of paper. She squirmed as he grabbed the chain from around his neck and pulled up a medallion with a familiar tricolored stone. With one glance at the necklace, Stella doubled her efforts to throw him off balance, but his arm was like steel. He squeezed her to him until she got a second dose of his stench. He managed to keep one hand on both the medallion and the slip of paper.

When she heard the Celtic words, she squeezed her eyes and shouted, "No. Let me go. We can wait for Finn."

The wind picked up as if in response to his words, and she twisted in his grip to monitor the ocean and the sky.

The fog was coming. So fast. Too fast.

In the distance, she heard the slamming of a car door. Isaiah? He must have broken speed limits the whole way. She stared at the fog, felt the pounding of the man's heart against her back as he pulled her closer.

Isaiah wouldn't reach her in time.

The world went silent as the fog enveloped her in bright, white light.

THANK YOU FOR READING

I sincerely hope you enjoyed reading, *European Stone Vacation* and getting a sneak peak into Stella's adventure.

A STONE DENIED
Available Now

Want to know when my next book is available?
Sign up for my newsletter at www.kimallred.com.

As an additional thank you for signing up for my newsletter, a free copy of *A Legacy of Stone* is available for download. This prequel to the *Mórdha Stone Chronicles* introduces Lily Mayfield, the last Keeper of Stones...until AJ that is!

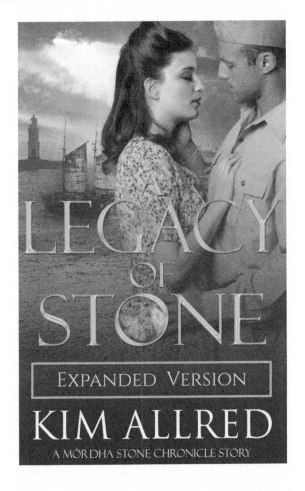

ABOUT THE AUTHOR

Kim Allred lives in an old timber town in the Pacific Northwest where she raises alpacas, llamas and an undetermined number of free-range chickens. Just like AJ and Stella, she loves sharing stories while sipping a glass of fine wine or slurping a strong cup of brew.

Her spirit of adventure has taken her on many journeys including a ten-day dogsledding trip in northern Alaska and sleeping under the stars on the savannas of eastern Africa.

Kim is currently working on the final books for the Mórdha Stone Chronicles series and the next books in her sizzling romance series—Masquerade Club.

For more books and updates:
www.kimallred.com

facebook.com/kim.allred.52831

instagram.com/kimallredauthor

bookbub.com/authors/kim-allred

amazon.com/-/e/B07CQY2J8Y

Made in United States
Orlando, FL
07 April 2023

31852418R00125